I0549144

Savannah J

Raising Tristan

By Savannah J

Savannah J

Raising Tristan

This book is a work of fiction. Places, events and, situations in this story are purely fictional. Any resemblance to actual persons, living or dead are coincidental.

Copyright 2013 by Savannah J. All rights reserved.

No part of this book may be reproduced, stored in a retrieval system, or transmitted by any means, electronic, mechanical, photocopying, recording, or otherwise, without written permission from the author.

ISBN-13: 978-0-9889075-0-8

Cover and model's photography by, J. Mikes Photography, LLC

Cover model, JaMontae Holmes

Author photo by, Maurice Howard of Uzuri Images

Printed in the United States of America by AA Printing
813-886-0065

Savannah J

Raising Tristan

From the desk of Savannah J:

We as a society so often pay homage to our single mothers out there holding it down. Many are raising boys on their own without the help of a man. What we often fail to do as a group however, is acknowledge our single fathers. The men who not only choose to step up to the plate and take responsibility for their offspring, but take it a step further by assuming full custody and care.

It is these noble men who go quietly about the business of raising their children that are so often overlooked. We see them out and about spending time and doing their best to meet needs. We automatically think there is a woman somewhere near by, when often there is not.

Please join me in applauding these men and their efforts to be great fathers. If you know any single fathers personally; I know I do, reach out to them and let them know they are not alone. Perhaps you can baby sit or take them a meal or even run an errand or two. Let's come together and make ourselves as accessible to our single fathers as we do our single moms.

Ciao!

Acknowledgements

To Jehovah God, my Lord and Savior. I can never praise and thank you enough for all of the blessing you have given me. You are the beat of my heart and the air that I breathe. Thank you for blessing me with the gift of writing.

My son, J. Michael, you are still my greatest blessing. Thank you for reminding me, the good stuff is just around the corner. I am so proud of you, my Photographer Extraordinaire.

To the Savannah J Publications, LLC Dream Team, I thank you for your undying support and for never saying no, whenever I need you.

To my siblings, sister-in-law, and nieces and nephews, I thank you for always keeping it real with me whenever the need arises. My mentor, Brian W. Smith, I thank you for leading by example, and for making yourself available to answer my questions. Your wisdom is invaluable. P.S. thank you for asking me tough questions whenever I need to think before I act. Blessings!

To my cousin Glenda, thank you for becoming a part of my team and for lending me your expertise. Chantel, I thank you for lending me your beauty and for being ready to take to the roads whenever I need you.

To the BBQR Family, thank you for loving me, boasting on me and supporting me always. My classmates from WHS Class of 1974, thank you for your "Ride or Die" friendship, for supporting me and always making me feel special. Tammy, I still thank you for insisting, I finish Toward the Light. Look where your push has gotten me. My book club, The Natural Woman Book Club, every time we read one of my books, I feel so special. Thanks ladies! Maurice Howard, your friendship and expertise are invaluable, thank you.

To my readers, thanks for not only reading my work but loving it. You make it all worthwhile. Dr. George C. Longest thanks for seeing the writer in me. And to Doddie, the fixer of my broken wing, I'm still making good decisions for me. Thank you for your guidance.

To anyone I should have thanked but forgot, please charge it to my head and not my heart.

Savannah J

Dedication: *To Alex and single fathers everywhere.*

Savannah J

Raising Tristan

Savannah J

Prologue

Moselle stood facing the man who in a matter of minutes would become her husband. As she heard the minister speaking her full name expecting her to repeat after him, she did so on autopilot.

"I, Moselle Renae Laveau . . ." As the words left her mouth, her eyes never left her intended. She took in the full features of his face. The way soft lines framed his brown eyes as he smiled, the length of his nose speaking to his Creole heritage and his full lips that left her breathless so many times when he kissed her.

Still, she wondered how she had gotten there. How had this man come into her life so unexpectedly and swept her off her feet. He was not the type of man she anticipated spending her life with.

He wasn't a doctor or accountant or a shirt-and-tie kind of guy; yet, he was all she'd ever wanted. On any given day she would have passed him by, but something about him made it impossible to walk away.

When she heard the familiar voice of his son, her focus momentarily shifted to the front pew where the boy sat with her future in-laws. Moselle couldn't help but smile.

Shiloh beamed at his fiancé making eye contact with his son. He couldn't believe she was really standing face to face with him pledging her love for eternity. He gently squeezed her diminutive hand drawing her attention back to him.

There was a period of time in their relationship when he surmised things between them were over. But the bond between them prevailed, and now she was becoming his wife.

"By the power and authority invested in me by God and the State of Louisiana, I now pronounce you husband and wife together. Shiloh, you may salute your bride."

As Shiloh pulled Moselle into his arms, he felt as though he was in a fairytale. His life was finally perfect. He had finally arrived. "I love you Mo," he whispered into her lips as he kissed his new wife.

"I love you more," she answered. When they finally pulled away from one another and faced the congregation, the applause was thunderous.

Shiloh scooped his son into his left arm and used his right arm to draw Mo to him. They were now a family and he knew God had blessed him with more than he'd ever dreamt possible.

The Beginning

Shiloh gripped Angela's hips pulling them higher, closer to his pelvis. His thrusts became more forceful as he felt himself nearing release. He'd already pleased her twice and now it was his turn.

Although, Angela was nothing more than a regular booty call, Shiloh made sure she got hers. "Shhhhh . . ." he breathed out, as the air was forced from his lungs during his climax.

When he was finished, he rolled off her and pulled her to his chest. He didn't love her but he loved to cuddle. Since he didn't have a girlfriend, for now, Angela would have to do.

Shiloh closed his eyes and allowed the sweet euphoric feeling that always followed their intimate moments to wash over him. He was just about to drift off to sleep when Angela's voice pulled him back.

"I'm pregnant."

He frowned. "What did you say?"

"I said I'm pregnant." Her voice sounded flat to him.

He took a minute to turn to her. Cupping her chin with his hand, he pulled her face towards his. "How far?" He didn't doubt for a second the baby was his.

"Three months . . . I don't want it." Angela looked him directly in the eyes when she uttered those words.

Shiloh sat up on the side of the bed; this time he kept his back to her. "What are you saying, Angie? It's a little late to get an abortion, don't you think?"

"Not if I lie."

He stood slowly to his feet. His six foot three inch, 200 pound frame seemed to rise in deliberate motion to Angela. She'd never been afraid of or uncomfortable around Shiloh until now.

"Are you telling me you're going to kill my baby? He has a heartbeat Angela. His heart is beating . . . How can you do that?" His eyes narrowed as he spoke.

"I never wanted kids; you know that. And what we have isn't exactly a relationship . . . we're—"

"Don't say it," he snapped, cutting her off. Shiloh hated it when she used the 'F' word followed by 'buddy' to describe their relationship. He knew they weren't a couple, but to him they were more than that.

Angela stood to her feet as well. She slowly made her way to the bathroom. Although her pregnancy wasn't very far along, the baby still pressed on her bladder. After relieving herself, she turned on the shower.

When she finished, she dried off and got dressed. She grabbed her purse and car keys and headed down the stairs. Before she could open the door to Shiloh's home to leave, he placed his hand against it stopping her.

"This ain't over Angie." He spoke close to her ear. "You hear me? This conversation is far from over."

"It's over for tonight," she replied softly.

"Perhaps, that's so. But you better believe I'll be by tomorrow to finish this. You ain't killin' my boy."

Angela remained quiet. All she wanted to do was go home and lay down. She knew there was no winning this argument at this point. She'd sleep on it and come up with a strategy in the morning to ensure she had her way; even if it meant disappearing.

Chapter 1

Five months later

"Damm, this shit hurt!" Angela yelled. She grabbed her swollen belly. "I know I should ah' got rid of this one just like the rest. But no, I had to listen to yo stupid ass!"

Shiloh reached for her hand to comfort her, but she recoiled from his touch. He sighed. "Babies are a gift Angie."

"Ah' gift to who? You ain't the one layin' up here in labor," she hissed.

"They can give you something for the pain soon and you can get that epidural too."

"Oh god!" she said before vomiting all over herself and the bed. Before Shiloh could place the basin under her chin, she finished on the floor.

Shiloh shook his head before he spoke. "Angie, I'm here for you . . . all you have to do is to tell me when you feel sick. That's the second time you've done that."

"I don't give a —." A contraction caught her mid sentence before she could hurl another insult his way. It seemed like a blessing to Shiloh.

"Let me go tell the nurses you're sick, so they can get you straight."

Once in the hall, he leaned against the wall and took a deep breath. This wasn't the way he envisioned his first child coming into the world. It was supposed to be with a woman he loved and who loved him back.

He didn't for one minute fail to take full responsibility for his actions. Shiloh knew he should have donned a condom every time they were together. How many times had friends and cousins, for that matter, ended up pregnant because they took a chance?

"It only takes one time, man," His cousin Boo-Boo told him following the birth of Boo's little girl. *"Don't be like me and end up with a baby by somebody who makes your life, hell."*

Shiloh rubbed his eyes and mumbled, "Why didn't I listen to you, Boo-Boo?"

"Are you okay?"

The sound of Karen, Angela's nurse, pulled him from his thoughts. "No, she threw up again . . . all over herself and the floor."

"Well, let's get her cleaned up" Karen said, as though she wasn't bothered at all.

"Listen," Shiloh started, "I apologize for her behavior and the mess. For some reason, she won't tell me when she feels sick."

Just then the call bell to Angela's room went off. Karen and Shiloh both could hear her screaming something into the speaker.

"I'll go on in," he said softly.

Thirty minutes later, Karen with Shiloh's help had Angela cleaned up and repositioned in bed. Much to Shiloh's delight, it was time for Angie to have more pain medicine and the anesthesiologist was on his way to give her an epidural - a double plus for Shiloh.

With her pain under control, Angela was a little less obnoxious. But she still seemed to take pleasure in mistreating Shiloh.

Savannah J

The nurses had changed shift for the night and the new nurse on duty was named Moriah. Shiloh appreciated her direct manner with the situation. Karen was good in his mind but Moriah was older and more of the motherly type.

He leaned back in his chair and at the advice of the nurse attempted to catch a nap. After what seemed about only 15 minutes, he heard his name being called.

"Shiloh . . . Shiloh . . . wake up. Angela's ready to push." He jumped to his feet, somewhat disoriented until the nurses in the room helped him calm down by explaining what to expect.

He didn't know if it was fear of the unknown or just plain fear, but Angela suddenly seemed grateful for his help.

The baby was born three hours later and just as Shiloh thought, it was a boy. What happened next caused him to feel as if he'd been sucked into a vortex.

His son was early and small. Although he cried at birth, he had to be taken to an intensive care unit for babies. The doctors allowed him to hold his son for a few minutes. When Shiloh attempted to place the baby in Angie's arms, she turned her head and refused to even look at her son.

Chapter 2

Moriah showed Shiloh to the waiting area where he could sit until he was able to visit his son. Unlike most new families who bond, Angela didn't want him anywhere near her after the baby was born.

He sat in the waiting room all alone wishing his parents were with him. Taking his phone from the holster, he called his mother. She picked up on the second ring.

"Hi sweetie!" His mother almost sang into the receiver. "Is the baby here?"

"Yes, Mom, he is."

"Oh my, it's a boy?! We have a grandson Robert!" She yelled to Shiloh's father.

"How much did he weight son?"

"I don't know?"

"What is it, Shiloh? Is something wrong with the baby?" Ines Milner, Shiloh's mother, knew her son very well and she could hear the dejection in his voice.

"Well, he was a little early and so he's small. They took him to the NIC-unit. I'm waiting for them to come and get me so I can see him."

Ines was silent for a minute. "And what else is bothering you, because that's not all."

"I'm good."

"Shiloh, you know the one thing you could never get away with was lying to me. So what is it?"

"Mom, how did I get here? How did I allow myself at age 41 to get tangled up in a mess? And now I've brought an innocent life into the fold."

His mother resisted the urge to say, *I told you so*, instead she did what any mother would do at that moment. She reassured her son.

"Listen, Shiloh. Anybody at any time can get themselves into a jam. It has nothing to do with age. Your dad and I raised you in the church and gave you a good foundation but that doesn't mean you won't make mistakes."

"Angie was so ugly during her labor and after . . . she didn't even want me in the room after they took the baby away."

"Where are you now?" Ines's heart broke for her son.

"I'm in the waiting room they have here."

Ines sighed. "Son, yes you made a mistake but the baby isn't a mistake; he's a blessing. Now your relationship with Angela is another story."

Shiloh primped his lips and shook his head. "Okay mom, just say what you have to say."

"You have a calling on your life son and you've spent most of your adult years running from it."

"Well, you can't run away from God." He finished her sentence for her. "I know Mom, I know. What has that got to do with Angela?"

"What does that have to do with Angela? I don't believe you asked me such ah' thing! Anyway, that's not important right now. What's important is you and that little boy."

"Mom! The nurse is here to get me," Shiloh told his mother after looking up and seeing a nurse smiling at him.

They said their quick goodbyes with Shiloh promising to call with an update.

"Hi. Are you Mr. Milner?"

"Yes," Shiloh replied rising to his feet.

"I'm Cindy; one of the Newborn Intensive Care Unit (NICU) nurses. Are you ready to see your son?"

"I sure am," he answered. For the first time in three days, Shiloh smiled.

Cindy led Shiloh to the unit and showed him where to wash his hands and where the gowns were kept for him to wear during his visits.

The one kind thing Angela had done for him was to give him the ID band that allowed him to visit the baby at will. When Shiloh finally laid eyes on his son, a profound feeling of love overtook him swelling his heart and eyes with tears.

Cindy took her time and explained everything going on with the baby. When she asked him what his son's name was, Shiloh gave her a puzzled look. He realized he and Angela had never discussed a name.

"It's okay," Cindy said, "You and his Mom have time to do name picking."

"Yeah, I guess . . ." Shiloh responded.

"Well, I'll leave you alone for a visit with your son," Cindy said, before stepping away.

Raising Tristan

Once they were alone, Shiloh touched his son's little hands and face. He took his time and explored every inch of his son, marveling in the satiny feel of his skin. When he was satisfied, he decided to go and check on Angela.

"Even though she's nasty, it doesn't mean I have to follow suit," He thought to himself.

Chapter 3

Shiloh made his way to the unit where Angela was recovering. He found out her room number, took a deep breath and knocked.

"Come in."

He opened the door and walked slowly over to the bed. "I saw the baby. He's beautiful . . . he has a head full of hair and your eyes."

Angela closed her eyes and turned her face away from Shiloh.

"Don't you want to see him Angie? He's little and has one of those oxygen tubes on his nose. Other than that, he looks good." His tone sounded disheartened.

(Silence)

"Angela, don't do this."

"Do what?" She snapped at him.

"Ignore me . . . ignore him."

Finally she faced him. "I told you in the beginning, I didn't want kids. When we started hanging out, I made that clear. You agreed."

Shiloh pulled up a chair beside her. "You're right, I did. And we used condoms every time except for those two days we went out of town.

I told you I didn't have any on me and got ready to find a store. You stopped me, Angela. You said it didn't matter; that you'd just had your period."

She looked at him but didn't respond.

"You enjoyed me that weekend as much as I enjoyed you. As a matter of fact you said it was the best."

"What is your point?" She hissed.

"You're acting as if this is my entire fault, as if I made him by myself; that's my point."

This time Angela glared at Shiloh. Her eyes filled with tears and she quickly brushed them away. "I don't want to see him." She snapped again.

"He's your son."

"No, he's not. He's yours," she said in a whisper through broken words.

Shiloh felt as if Angela had hit him in the stomach with a 2x4. The air left his body so quickly it knocked him back into the chair. He grabbed his head in an attempt to quell the dizziness that overtook him and regain his composure.

"He's a baby Angela. How can you be so cruel? How can you live with yourself?" He said through clinched teeth.

Just as the words left his mouth, Angela's nurse came into the room to check on her and give her pain medicine. After she left, Shiloh stood to leave too. "We have to name him," he said quietly.

"You pick it," was her only response. With that, she closed her eyes and allowed the medicine to lull her to sleep.

Shiloh stopped by the NICU once more to see his son before going home to rest. He held the tiny baby's hand and quietly said a prayer and vowed to always be there and care for his son no matter what.

"We'll name him tomorrow," he said to his baby's nurse on his way out.

Raising Tristan

As Shiloh walked to his car, he decided to phone his mother in the morning and ask her and his father to drive up from Virginia Beach, Virginia to Richmond; he needed some backup. *"If Angela chooses to be a butt hole,"* he thought to himself, *"that doesn't mean I have to."* He knew he couldn't get through these next few weeks alone.

Chapter 4

Early the next morning Shiloh called his job to explain the situation and told them he'd be in later. Next, he called his parents and asked them to come to Richmond as soon as possible. Even if just for a few days, he could use the support.

Shiloh Michel Milner hailed from New Orleans, Louisiana. He'd moved to Richmond in 2005 following the devastation caused by Hurricane Katrina on the city of New Orleans and the surrounding area. Although he'd been a resident of Richmond for quite a few years, he still didn't have many friends in the area. He chose to keep to himself and concentrate on making a successful life.

He dated a few women over the years but no one he wanted to settle down with. Shiloh's relationship with Angela was purely for companionship and sexual gratification - nothing more. Although he'd made excuses and justified their relationship in his mind, he never regretted it, that is, until now.

As he climbed into his 1998 BMW 740i, he paused for a minute and thought about his past. Once again, he asked himself exactly how he had gotten to this place in his life. Shiloh loved children and always wanted a few of his own, just not like this.

On a whim, he picked up his cell phone and called his cousin Louis aka Boo-Boo. Boo picked up on the third ring.

"Talk to me cuz," he said in his heavy southern accent.

"What's up, man? How you doin'?" Shiloh asked. It was obvious he and his cousin were close. The joy resonated in his voice.

"I'm good man, I'm good. To what do I owe this early morning call?"

Shiloh knew even though it was already ten o'clock in the morning, Boo-Boo was still in bed. "Angie had a baby last night; I have a son."

Boo Boo frowned and sat straight up in bed. "Say what?"

"I said I have a son; he was born last night."

"Word! You got seed cuz?!"

Shiloh paused and took a deep breath. "He's a baby man, not a plant. What is it with you and this seed mess?"

Boo-Boo could hear the disgust in his cousin's voice. "It's just a sayin' man, just a sayin'."

"Well, could you drop the sayin' and refer to my son as a son, or boy or baby or—"

"Got it man . . . got it." Boo said, cutting Shiloh off.

"Good. You know I hate that. We are not seeds; we're people."

"Ohhhhkay! I said I got it Shiloh. Now tell me about my new cousin."

The two men chatted for about 30 minutes - the amount of time it took Shiloh to get to the hospital. Once he arrived, he bid his cousin goodbye and headed into the building. He decided to stop by Angela's room first and check on her.

When he walked into the room, he found the bed empty and clean and the room set up for the next patient. None of Angela's belongings were anywhere to be found.

Instead of panicking, he decided to step into the hall and ask the nurses if Angie had been moved. "Excuse me?" He said to the unit secretary, "Angela Pitchard, has she been moved to another room?"

The young lady behind the desk looked at the computer screen in front of her. She knew early that morning, in a flurry of drama, Angela had checked herself out Against Medical Advice (AMA), but she wanted to appear professional.

She looked up and Shiloh perceived before the young lady spoke something was wrong. "Mr. Milner, may I have you wait in the lounge for our nurse manager? She will be right with you."

"Is something wrong with Angie?" Shiloh felt his chest begin to tighten. His intuition jumped into overdrive, something he'd inherited from his Creole great-great-grandmother, and he struggled to shut it down.

"Ummm, no nothing's wrong with her, it's just that . . . Mr. Milner please just have a seat and wait for my manager. She'll explain everything."

If the unit secretary hadn't looked as if she would wet her pants at any moment, Shiloh would have grilled her for an answer. He knew his height along with his piercing eyes could be intimidating, and so instead of pressing the situation, he turned and headed to the lounge.

No sooner than he sat down, two women entered the lounge. "Mr. Milner? I'm Lucy, the Mother-Newborn Unit Nurse Manager. And this is Charell, our Nurse Case Manager." Both women extended their hands.

Lucy took no time before she jumped right in. "Ms. Pitchard checked herself out of the hospital early this morning." She paused as if she were giving Shiloh time to respond.

"What do you mean she checked herself out; she just had a baby."

This time Charell spoke up. "It's called Against Medical Advice; AMA is the acronym we use."

"I know what AMA means," Shiloh shot back. "Why didn't someone call me? We have a child together for goodness sake."

"Mr. Milner, Ms. Pitchard strongly insisted she did not want you called. But we did try to call you from the NICU to find out when you'd be in."

Shiloh pulled his phone from his side and glanced at it. In his haste to get to the hospital, he had neglected to check for missed calls. "I guess I didn't hear my phone," he said. He willed himself to calm down.

"That's okay Mr. Milner," Charell said. She paused and then continued. "Let me explain what transpired."

Raising Tristan

Lucy and Charell filled Shiloh in on the situation involving Angie just as it transpired leaving no stone unturned. Although their delivery manner was professional, it was clear Angela had made a scene worthy of a book.

When they finished, Shiloh leaned back in his chair and tried to absorb what was said.

"Are you telling me she abandoned our baby?" He asked disbelievingly.

"Yes, sir, that is exactly what I'm saying but she gave you temporary emergency custody," Charell said. She handed him the paperwork. "I will need your signature saying you'll accept temporary custody of the baby."

Shiloh's head snapped to attention. "Baby? He's my Son."

"Mr. Milner," Lucy started in a soothing tone, "Because you and the baby's mother are not married, we cannot take your word for paternity. She did name you as the father, but once the baby is released, you will have to prove parenthood since you've only been granted temporary guardianship."

Shiloh felt his chest tighten even more. He sighed and looked down at his hands. *"What have I gotten myself into Father-God,"* he whispered to himself.

After a few seconds he looked up. "May I still see him whenever I want?"

"You sure may. As a matter of fact, when the baby is discharged, he'll more than likely go home with you," Charell said.

Shiloh's look told her he didn't care for his son being referred to as 'the baby,' and so she added, "As soon as you name him, I will personally see to it that everyone uses the name you've chosen."

For the first time in a long time, Shiloh felt inadequate as a man. He closed his eyes briefly and asked God for strength.

"I think I want to call him, Tristan Isaiah."

"Then, Tristan Isaiah it is!" Lucy exclaimed with a smile.

When Shiloh finally entered the NICU he felt as though he'd just run a marathon. The nurse assigned to Tristan's care for the morning shift informed him that his son was stable enough to hold if he wanted.

For the second time in the past few days Shiloh smiled again. Although he was worn down by Angie's antics, holding Tristan gave him a second wind.

Chapter 5

The following morning at exactly six o'clock, Shiloh heard his father's signature knock on his door. It didn't matter that he had a door bell; Shiloh's dad always knocked.

He'd once explained to Shiloh that in his experience people in a deep sleep would respond to a loud rapt on the door faster than the ringing of a bell. Robert Milner, a retired police captain, had awakened many a family in the middle of the night - more than he cared to number.

"How's my little man!" Ines exclaimed as she pulled Shiloh into a bear hug once he opened the front door.

"I'm well Mom," he responded giving her the eye for referring to him as a child. "But believe it or not, I'm actually a man now."

"Son." Robert Milner embraced his son as well and Shiloh leaned into the hug as if to draw from his father's strength.

"Well," Ines said moving toward the kitchen with a small cooler in her hand, "Help your father unload the car, and I'll put on the coffee and grits."

A feeling of calm assurance spread over Shiloh's heart as he turned and followed his father to the car. He knew when his mother headed for the kitchen to make her **legendary** coffee and New Orleans style breakfast, everything would be alright.

Ines Milner was gifted with the ability to problem solve even the most challenging problems. That, along with her ability to remain calm even in the most daunting situations was what attracted Robert to her.

After a breakfast of grillades and grits with Parmesan cheese, orange juice and coffee, Inez was ready to listen to Shiloh explain how he ended up a single father.

Chapter 6

"You mean to tell me she just walked out on her baby?" Robert asked after listening to his son.

"Yes dad; that's exactly right."

"Well, have you gone over to where she lives to ask her why she abandoned her son?" Robert continued to probe as if he found it difficult to believe Angela had disappeared.

"I sure did . . . she's gone Dad. She told me she never wanted kids and I guess she meant it. But Tristan still has me, and he has you and Mom."

"I don't have time or energy to waste looking for her. She knows where I live and if she wants any contact with Tristan, she knows where to find him." Shiloh added.

"Tristan Isaiah, I like that. Don't you like that, Robert? He has your middle name." Ines said.

Shiloh and Ines could tell by Robert's expression the last thing on his mind was the baby's name.

"Leave it be Rob." Ines said, reading her husband's mind. "If the girl is that trifling, do we really want her around our grandbaby? Good riddance to her."

"Mom's right dad. Please don't call any of your buddies and ask for help tracking Angie down. Now that you two are here, I know I have support and with your help. I can do this."

Robert sat back in the overstuffed wing chair he occupied and folded his arms across his chest. His belly was as flat and his body as lean as the day he married Ines Antoinette Bedeau.

They met on the campus of Southern University at New Orleans. Both wanted to attend college out of state but their families could not afford to send them. At the time when Robert began to date Ines, he knew he could not afford to give her much. But he vowed to one day provide her with all her heart desired.

Raising Tristan

Ines was instantly attracted to Robert with his rich dark chocolate complexion and wavy hair. Her coloring bordered more on that of honey and she knew her parents would never approve her dating someone with skin darker than hers. The deeper she fell in love with Robert Milner, the less she cared what her parents thought.

Ines' eyes were a deep blue, inherited from her paternal great grandmother, Ines Antoinette Meilleur-Bedeau, for whom she was named. Grand-mere Meilleur-Bedeau was said to have moved to Baltimore shortly after her sixteenth birthday to find work to send money home to help her family. In order to find the best employment available at that time, she is said to have passed for White.

Robert looked from his son's face back to his wife's. He realized they were correct in what they were saying, but it disturbed him deeply to know his first born grandson would grow up in a single parent home.

Ines smiled, once again reading her husband's thoughts. "Don't worry Rob; Shiloh will not be raising our grandbaby alone. He is about to meet someone very special."

"Mom!" Shiloh shot her a look. "How do you know I want someone in my life right now? My focus is going to be on raising Tristan. I've had enough with the dating scene."

"Well—"

"Ines! Don't start with that spooky stuff. You know I hate it when you do that," Robert said cutting her off.

"Okay," Ines answered. "But . . ."

"Tell you what," Shiloh interjected, "How about we go see the baby. And then Mom, you can help me pick out what all I'm going to need to take care of Tristan once he comes home."

"Perfect idea," Ines said as she jumped up and grabbed her purse. "It's not too early to get into the unit is it?" She asked in after thought.

"No, we have twenty-four-hour visitation. Let me grab my keys and I'll be ready." He winked his eye at his father when his mother headed toward the door.

Thank you was written all over Robert's face.

Chapter 7

Ines' face beamed with pride as she looked into the face of her first born grandson. She hadn't felt this much love since she looked at Shiloh for the first time.

"Now how long does he have to keep the oxygen?" She asked Tristan's nurse.

"Probably not much longer; his blood levels are pretty good." Cindy answered. She was now Tristan's primary nurse. "By the way," she added, "Our nurse practitioner is on today; she would like to talk with you about your baby's progress. No one has spoken with you since his admission, right?"

"That's correct. I'd love to speak with her." Shiloh replied.

As Cindy went to notify the nurse practitioner of the Milner family's arrival, Shiloh turned to his mother. "Mom, remember Tristan is my son and I'm perfectly capable of asking pertinent questions. So let me handle this - okay?"

Ines primped her lips and rolled her eyes. "Mom . . ." he repeated.

"Fine" Ines curtly answered.

"Thanks mother," Shiloh said and kissed her on the cheek eliciting a huge smile.

"Shouldn't your father be in here? After all, he'll be helping with the baby too."

"Two at the bedside at a time Mom, we can fill him in."

Chapter 8

Moselle approached Shiloh and his mother from the front of the NICU. Shiloh looked up and smiled when he saw her and stood to his feet.

"Mr. Milner? Hi, I'm Moselle Laveau. I'm the nurse practitioner working with the Neonatologist today. It is a pleasure to meet you. Your young man is doing great."

Shiloh took her outstretched hand into his and shook it. As he smiled down at Moselle, she had to concentrate to hear his words. She couldn't help but think to herself that Shiloh looked as if someone had dipped him into a vat of dark gourmet chocolate, because the popular brand never made anything that fine.

Ines smiled to herself as she witnessed the exchange between the two. Her son didn't realize it yet, but he was shaking the hand of his future wife. Once Ines shook Moselle's hand and felt her spirit, *she* knew everything was going to be alright.

Tristan's course in the NICU went smoothly. Once Moselle and the doctors were satisfied with his progress, plans were put in place for discharge. It took a couple of weeks for Tristan and Shiloh to get the hang of bottle feeding, but the nurses in the unit were extremely supportive. Shiloh looked forward to spending time with his son, but he also looked forward to seeing Moselle.

He wanted to ask her out badly, but he knew that would be an improper move. A part of him doubted she'd say yes; after all he was just a mechanic. But little did he know that Moselle felt the same way about him.

Each night after work she'd phone her best friend, Tangy, and talk endlessly about Shiloh. "Girl, he is such a good father. He is in the unit for about two hours in the morning and comes back every night after work for about three hours. Did I mention he's fine?"

"Only about a bazillion times . . ." Tangy would reply before laughing with Moselle about it.

"He's going be discharged in a few days," she said. This time Moselle's tone was not as upbeat as it usually was.

"Mo, why don't you tell him how you feel? I mean the baby's going home and it's not like you're his pediatrician or anything. You will probably never see him again after they walk out those doors."

"I could lose my job Tangy; you know that."

"Okay, lose your job how?" Tangy's tone had an edge to it that told Moselle she was about to be admonished.

"You know good and well how, Tangy. I cannot approach that man with my personal feelings about him. If my head doc finds out, I'm history."

"Why does he have to find out? You said the baby's going home in a couple days' right?"

Moselle sighed, "Yes I did."

"Well, when he stays the night all you have to do is spend some time with him. You have to meet with him anyway right? Before you leave the room, express your feeling to him. From what you've told me about him, Shiloh seems like a decent guy. I don't think he'll run and snitch."

"I guess . . ."

"Mo, this could be your future. Don't let him slip away."

Chapter 9

The day had finally come for Shiloh to spend the night taking complete care of Tristan. His parents had returned to Chesterfield to provide a hand once they came home. Robert would only be staying a couple days, but Ines would remain with Shiloh for two weeks.

It had been decided the Milner's would rent out their home in Virginia Beach and move to Chesterfield to assist with Tristan's care. Ines made it clear her grandson would not be attending daycare. Although Shiloh pretended to put up opposition, he was secretly pleased with the decision.

Tristan's nurse for the night got them settled in a room close to the unit. Once Shiloh and his mother were comfortable, she brought the baby in.

"I will be checking on you hourly, so please leave a light on," the nurse instructed. She also reviewed other safety issues with them before closing the door and leaving the new family alone.

"Wow, this is really it Mom," Shiloh said peering down at his sleeping son. Ines could tell by the tone of his voice he was wishing that Tristan's mother were around to see how beautiful the baby was.

She wanted to pour words of encouragement over her son, but instead she held her tongue knowing this situation would work itself out. Instead of speaking, she joined her son at the baby's bedside and hugged him.

"Why don't you get some rest son? I'll take the first feeding tonight and the 6 a.m. or 7 a.m. feeding tomorrow morning."

Shiloh frowned. "You mean I gotta do the middle of the night feeds?"

"Ummmm hummm." Ines replied. She worked hard to contain the laughter bubbling up inside her.

"Grand-mere is sending me to boot camp, lil' man," Shiloh said as he picked up his sleeping son. "But I don't mind, because you know, daddy loves you so much. I'd do anything for you."

Shiloh placed the sleeping baby on his chest and lay across the bed fully dressed. It seemed as though only seconds had passed before Ines heard the soft snores of her son. She looked at the man who was once the baby she'd cradled in the same manner. It seemed like only yesterday.

At nine o'clock the next morning, Moselle knocked on the door of Shiloh's room. When it opened and she stood face to face with Ines, she had to work quickly to hide her disappointment. But Ines, being Ines, picked up on it right away.

"Come on in; my son is in the shower. Do you need to check on the baby?"

Moselle stood right outside the bathroom door. She could hear the water running in the shower and Shiloh's rich baritone voice singing a song by *Brian McKnight*. It was easy for her to visualize the water on his smooth skin, and she secretly wished she could be his towel.

"No," Moselle said, remembering why she'd come to his room. "I don't need the baby yet. I just wanted to go over a few things with Mr. Milner before Dr. Grant discharges Tristan."

"Well," Ines smiled, "I will have Shiloh call you once he's out of the shower. How's that?"

"Perfect." Moselle turned and left the room before she made a further fool of herself. Try though she may, she knew her attraction to Shiloh had not gone unnoticed by Mrs. Milner.

"I'm going for breakfast," Ines informed her son once he stepped from the bathroom. He had put on a pair of shorts after his shower; his mother knew he needed to get dressed.

"Shall I bring you something or should we take turns going down to get sometime to eat so someone can watch the baby?" She continued.

"Ummmm no," he answered. He knew the baby would awaken shortly for his morning bottle. "Just bring me some pancakes, eggs and turkey bacon."

"Oh, yes. The nurse practitioner, Moselle, would like for you to call her once you're dressed. She needs to talk with you before Tristan goes home this morning."

After he dressed and fed the baby, Shiloh phoned the unit for Moselle. When she walked in the door his breath was once again taken away by her appearance.

Her Café Au Lait hued skin, dark eyes and dark hair rendered her stunning in his eyes. There was also someone she reminded him of; he just couldn't put his finger on it.

Moselle had to catch herself to keep from uttering the words, *"umph, umph, umph"* that she thought to herself out loud when Shiloh opened the room door. His shorts and crewneck shirt hung perfectly on his muscular frame, and the cologne he wore ignited a flame that made her want a cold shower before she returned to the NICU.

"Uhhh, good morning," he said as he stepped aside so she could enter the room. "Please excuse the mess. We didn't really know what to bring," he added suddenly feeling self conscious about the space.

"Not a problem," Moselle said with a smile. "I don't have children of my own, but I have nieces and nephews who I care for from time to time and I work here."

Shiloh smiled. Something about her put him at ease. "Please have a seat," he said.

Moselle reviewed with him everything to expect from Tristan at home as a premature baby. She answered all his questions and did a quick exam on the baby. She also informed him a nurse would be in shortly to pick the baby up so that Dr. Grant and nursing could do a discharge physical.

As she turned to leave, Shiloh stopped her. "Excuse me; I just want to say thank you for all you've done for me and my son. Your kindness will always be appreciated."

"You are more than welcome; I'm just doing my job."

"I also want to say you look nice today." He smiled his million-dollar smile.

Moselle frowned and looked down at herself. "Well, thanks but I'm wearing scrubs. I do clean up nicely though."

Shiloh cocked his head to the side and regarded her. "I'd love to see that. I hope you don't think this forward of me or inappropriate, but I'd love to take you out for coffee and Jazz sometime. I know a great little place in Sandston."

"Oh my goodness!" Moselle screamed on the inside. *"Wait until I tell Tangy this!"* But aloud she said, "I'd like that," with her famous poker face.

"Let me give you my card," Shiloh said. "It has my office and cell numbers on it. Call me at your leisure. By the way, my cell is my home number. I don't have a land-line." He grinned.

Moselle glanced at the card and then him. "And what is that supposed to mean," she said sarcastically.

"Well, I have cousins who've told me that when a man gives only his cell number, it usually means he's trying to hide something. Well, I know you're aware I'm a single father, and why . . ."

Moselle smiled. "I'll give you a call on my next day off. And by the way, if I thought you were a dishonest man, I wouldn't even have entertained your conversation."

Raising Tristan

Just as Shiloh was about to say thank you, his mother tapped on the door and came in with his breakfast.

"I'll send Tristan's nurse right over so we can do his final examination and get you all out of here." Moselle said on her way out.

"Seems like a nice young lady," Ines said.

"Yes, and good at her job too," Shiloh added before he stuffed his mouth with pancakes, signaling to his mother that he had no intention of discussing Moselle with her.

Chapter 10

Tristan was home for nearly a week before Moselle called Shiloh. He had almost given up on her call when late one night his cell phone rang.

"Hey Shiloh, it's Moselle. How are you and how is your son?"

"He's great and low maintenance to hear my mother tell it," he said with a chuckle that was more of a sigh.

"I take it you beg her difference?"

"Yes, as a matter of fact, I do. But I guess it's because I'm pretty tired as most new parents are. Anyway, he's gained some weight and he eats pretty good. So, I presume, we aren't doing too badly."

"How long will your mother be with you?"

"She'll be here another two weeks and then she and my father are going to rent their home in Virginia Beach and move up here to help me with Tristan. My mother doesn't want him in daycare."

"Well, given that he's premature, that's actually not a bad idea and you won't have daycare costs."

"True . . . true" Shiloh said. "So, it's good to hear from you." He shifted the subject. Although Shiloh could talk about his son all day and night, he wanted to move the conversation toward a date. He was amazed that Moselle even called. After he'd given her his card, he only hoped to hear from her.

Although he knew he was an intelligent man and from a good family, he realized Moselle may think him beneath the caliber of men she usually dated. After all she was a Nurse Practitioner.

Little did he know his suspicions were right on. Moselle confided in Tangy prior to calling him. The men she was used to dating were professional, employed in white color positions, if you will.

"Girl, I'm not knocking the man, it's just that I want someone on my level," she said in a recent conversation with her best friend.

Moselle, how do you know he's not on your level? You haven't even spent any time with him," Tangy chided.

"Tangy, you know how important conversation is to me. What would we even have to talk about? We're from two different worlds."

"Okay, perhaps you're correct but you and that guy Boulder—"

"Stone." Moselle corrected.

"Stone, boulder what's the difference. He was an educated jerk."

Moselle was quiet for a minute.

"Give him a chance Mo, give yourself a chance. Live outside the box for once. You may be pleasantly surprised."

"I hope you're right about this, Tangy."

"Look, its just dinner Mo. It's not like you're going to marry the guy, right? Stop stressing and enjoy yourself. Don't you have enough stress with your job?"

"Yeah, I guess you're right. It has been awhile since I've been out on a date."

"Now, hang up this phone and call the man. Besides, my husband is due home any minute and I haven't seen him for a week."

"Ummmm hummmm. I see how this is workin', kickin' ya best friend to the curb for ya man." Moselle teased.

"Sho' you right."

Both women laughed and said their goodbyes. Moselle promised to call with an update once plans with Shiloh were firmed. As she talked with him that night, she began to feel a little bit better about seeing him.

"I have got to stop being so cynical," she thought to herself, as she listened to Shiloh's plans for their date, *"If I don't I'm going to end up alone."*

Chapter 11

Shiloh gave himself the once over before he stepped into the kitchen to kiss his son and mother goodbye prior to his date with Moselle.

"How do I look Mom?" He asked, knowing Ines would say he looked handsome just as she always did.

She smiled first and then looked down at Tristan who was asleep in her arms. "Your Daddy looks so handsome. He has a date tonight. What do you think of that?"

For a brief minute, Shiloh thought of Angie as he looked down at his son. He couldn't fathom for the life of him how she could just walk out on their baby. It was true he didn't love her, but he would have partnered with her in everyway to raise Tristan together.

He shook his head to release the thought and kissed his mother and son. "I won't be too late. We're going down to *Ty's Internet Café and Lounge* to listen to some jazz. One of the guys that works in the shop is playing tonight."

Ines smiled. "What does he play?"

"It's Murphy and he play's the sax."

"What kind of food do they serve? Anything Cajun?" Ines asked. She stood and made her way upstairs to lay the baby down and take a nap before he woke for his next bottle.

"They serve some cajun but not quite as good as home" he answered from the bottom of the stairs.

"Enjoy yourself and tell Moselle I said hello."

Shiloh frowned and then shook his head. He almost asked his mother how she knew he was going out with Moselle, but he already knew the answer to that one.

Instead he said, "See ya later Ma!" grabbed his keys and stepped into the night air.

Moselle insisted on meeting Shiloh at the restaurant since it was their first date. He consented only if she met him at the corner of Williamsburg Road and Wilson Street and allowed him to ride with her to park her car. He understood her reservations at him picking her up at her home, but he explained to her that a woman walking to the restaurant alone to meet him was unacceptable.

They arrived at *Ty's* about an hour before the show started. Shiloh planned it that way to give them time to talk without the noise level of the band.

"Are you familiar with Cajun food?" He asked at the risk of a look that said, *"Do I look that shallow to you?"* from his date.

"Well," Moselle started, "My parents are from New Orleans but my mother doesn't really cook Louisiana style food," she said as she perused the menu.

"Oh really?" Shiloh said.

"I've spent time in Louisiana, however, for medical conventions, so I'm somewhat familiar especially with the classics."

"Y'all didn't visit family?" He asked rather perplexed.

Moselle looked up from the menu "No, does that seem odd to you or something?"

"No it isn't odd at all. I apologize if I've insulted you in any way." Shiloh hoped he hadn't ruined the evening before it started.

Moselle smiled. "No worries," she said and turned her attention back to the menu. "What is Turducken? Now that that sounds interesting."

Well, if you really want my opinion, I think you should stick with the classics like Gumbo, Jambalaya, even the Crawfish Etouffee. Or maybe some Shrimp Creole and a lil' Cornbread."

"Sounds as if you're pretty familiar with the menu, have you been here before?" Moselle asked. She secretly wondered if Shiloh had brought another date to *Ty's* prior to her.

"Actually, I have. I come here for brunch every now and again after church. You see, I grew up in N'awlins."

"Oh my god, we could be related!" Moselle half joked with a big grin on her face.

Shiloh's brow furrowed. *"I hope not,"* he thought to himself.

"Just kidding!" Moselle reached out and playfully tapped him on the arm. "So, tell me what's good."

"Well," he started in an accent that sounded a lot like her father's now that she gave it some thought. "I don't think the staffs here are natives, but like I said, the classics here aren't too bad."

"Okay, what are you having?" She looked at him with eyes that said she was beginning to drop her guard.

"I'm going to have the Shrimp Creole tonight. It's not half bad."

Moselle decided on the same thing. After their food was served, she leaned into him. "So, do you know how to make authentic Cajun and Creole dishes?"

Shiloh smiled, "I sure do."

"Will you cook for me sometime?"

He softly touched her hand and silently thanked God for all the time his mother had him spend in the kitchen. "I'd love to."

After they finished their meal, Shiloh helped Moselle turn her chair toward the band. He didn't want to seem too forward on their first date but when she scooted a little closer and leaned against him, he gently slid his arm around her shoulder and smiled.

When her hand found its way to his knee, he knew this was going to be a good night and he would soon find himself in Moselle's company again.

Chapter 12

"'Mama, I think I found that girl... yay, yay, Mama, I think I found that girl.'" Shiloh came up behind his mother and wrapped his arms around her waist. He swayed from side to side singing an old Jackson 5 song.

His mother grinned, "So I take it you had a nice time last night?"

"Yes, I did," he answered. He grabbed a spoon and scooped a large helping of grits and cheese. "Mom, I am soooo happy you moved in with me!" He added through a mouth full.

Savannah J

"And exactly who is this young lady?" Robert Milner's voice boomed.

"Father, how nice of you to join us." Shiloh said to his dad ignoring Robert's attempt at being overbearing.

"Mother has made a lovely breakfast of sweet potato-pecan waffles, grits and my favorite, turkey bacon."

Robert stood with his hands folded across his chest with his signature scowl.

"And maple syrup." Shiloh held the bottle up for extra effect.

"Your mother was up all night long with the baby."

"I don't mind Robert and you know it," Ines said through pursed lips.

Shiloh put the syrup down and shook his head. "I was home by one o'clock Dad; it isn't like I was out all night. Why am I feeling like a teenager? I'm a grown man." He added in retrospect.

"Rob, don't start," Ines warned. "Your son is a very responsible man and you know this. Now, you have been overbearing for years. Not only is Shiloh a grown man but he now has a child of his own!"

"Mom, please . . . let's just eat," Shiloh attempted to stop the argument he saw brewing.

Ines put the dishcloth she had in her hand down. "No, not this time. Sit down Rob."

Robert remained silent and didn't budge. "I said sit down, now!" This time Ines raised her voice - something she rarely did.

On que, Robert sat and so did Shiloh. "For years you have hounded our son. You wanted him to be a man. You wanted him to be more responsible; you wanted him to be this, you wanted him to be that. Well, he *is* all that!"

She paused, "But what he isn't *is you*. He is his own person and his own man. And you *will not* come up here to Chesterfield and start this foolishness."

The room was so quiet you could have heard a pin drop. The tension in the air between Robert and Ines was so thick it made Shiloh extremely uncomfortable.

"I'm going to go and check on Tristan," he said in an attempt to leave the room.

"No you are not," his mother said. "You are going to sit there until this mess is settled once and for all because I've had enough." With that she turned her eyes on her husband.

Robert removed his glasses and ran his hand across his eyes. He knew his wife was on point in her thinking. He was disappointed that his son had brought a child into the world without being married. It didn't matter to him all of Shiloh's accomplishments, for some reason, all he saw were the failures.

When he looked into his wife's blue eyes, he saw the pain he had caused her over the years resulting from his relationship with his son. He knew that Ines Milner had truly reached her limit and if he coveted the relationship he had with her, he'd better start working on changing things between him and Shiloh.

"Son, when I was growing up we were pretty poor. But my parents did the best they could with what they had. Your grandfather wanted me to have more than he did; he wanted a better life for me and your aunts and uncles."

"Because of his vision for us, he sometimes pushed us too hard. It drove my sisters away and into the arms of men who were equally as demanding. My brothers and I all left home at the age of eighteen and never looked back."

"When I met your mother, I knew she was the one. My father's voice became even louder in my head. It became the driving force to my success so that your mother never had to work unless she wanted to."

"After you were born, I told myself I would never be like Grandpere, but . . . sometimes I think I'm worse." Robert's voice broke with his last words.

"Dad," Shiloh grabbed his father's hand. "You don't have to—"

"Yes I do," his father said dabbing his eyes with a napkin. "History repeats itself. If I don't begin the process of healing now, I promise, you will continue the cycle of . . . I don't even know what to call it," Robert said. His eyes met his wife's and she gave him a nod of approval.

"What your father is trying to say Son is he doesn't want you to drive Tristan the way he has you and his father did him. As the old saying goes, "'The buck stops here.'" Ines said as she held her son's hand.

She looked down at the circle formed by their hands. A scripture came to her mind from the book of Ecclesiastes 4:12b "A cord of three strands is not easily broken."

"How about we start with prayer," she said, "that's always the best place to start."

"Wait!" Shiloh said. He jumped up from the table and ran out of the room. He returned a few seconds later with a sleeping Tristan in his arms. He placed the baby in his carrier and sat him in the center of the table.

"Now the circle is complete. Now we can pray."

After family prayer and breakfast, Ines encouraged Robert and Shiloh to go for a drive and talk. She told them both she was more than capable of caring for a newborn. After all, she'd taken care of many a baby in her day.

Chapter 13

The next couple of months kept Shiloh very busy between work and his new son. His parents found a town home close by so that Ines could baby-sit during the day while Shiloh worked. She made it clear she would only spend the night incase of emergency.

His relationship with Moselle grew slowly, which suited him just fine. His main priority was caring for this son. With her work schedule and his single fatherhood, they spent time whenever they could.

Tristan would be turning three months in a few days, and Ines insisted on having cake and ice cream. Shiloh felt it would be the perfect time for Moselle to be formally introduced as the lady in his life.

"Hey baby. Got a question for you," he said one night over dinner. He'd cooked for her at her place while Ines babysat.

Moselle's eyes were closed and she had the most pleasant expression on her face. "Are you okay?" He asked when she didn't respond to his statement.

"Ummmm hummmm!" Mo said finally. "I am great. Baby; you put your big toe in this Etouffee!"

Shiloh's face took on a proud appearance. "See I told you crawfish were good. You just hadn't had it prepared by the best." He stuck his hands in the air.

"I must admit, you're exactly right. Okay, what was your question?" She put her fork down and faced him.

"Well, the only woman I've been dating is you, and I think I'm the only man you're seeing, right?"

"Yes, that's right." Moselle's curiosity got the best of her and she wondered where he was going with this.

Raising Tristan

Shiloh took her hand, "I'm kinda old fashioned, you know just ah' ole' country boy from N'awlins."

Moselle waited. "I was wondering if you would be my girl?" He asked.

She thought about the difference between them. Sure, Shiloh was sweet and they had a lot in common. She enjoyed his company but he was a single father and probably made a lot less money than she did. Even with all her thoughts as to why he couldn't possibly be the right one, her heart told her he was.

"I'd be honored," she finally answered.

Shiloh pulled her out of her chair and into his arms. He kissed her slowly and tenderly. His tongue found its way into her mouth, but it was a kiss that told her he was falling in love with *her* and not what was in her pants.

When he released her, his eyes confirmed what his lips had said.

"Tristan is going to be three months old in about five days. My Mother insists on giving him a little cake and ice cream party. I'd love to have you over and introduce you formally to my family," he said.

Moselle was a little taken aback. She knew it was a serious thing when a man, especially a self-proclaimed, old fashioned man took you home to meet his parents.

"If you think it's too soon or you're uncomfortable, I understand," he added.

"No, no I'm good. I guess I'm just surprised you want me to meet your family."

"Why wouldn't I? You're beautiful, intelligent and talented. Any man would be proud to have you on his arm and if he isn't, something's very wrong with him."

"Shiloh, we're getting ready to start Son." Ines' voice summoned him into the kitchen. "She'll be here; maybe she got caught in traffic."

"You're right," he said and kissed his mother on the cheek. In the back of his mind he hoped Moselle hadn't stood him up.

The plan for the afternoon was to have Tristan dedicated as well as celebrate his three months of life. The family was assembled in the back yard since it was a beautiful fall day. With the help of aunts and cousins that lived in the Maryland, Virginia and North Carolina area, Ines had decorated the yard beautifully. The women spent all day Saturday cooking while the men in the family picked up rental tables and chairs and then set them up according to Ines' specifications.

Raising Tristan

Shiloh asked his cousin Boo-Boo to be Tristan's god-father. As crazy as Boo was, Shiloh knew he would be there in a heart beat should he or the baby need him. His auntie Cecile stood as the godmother. Although she was his aunt, they were more like sister and brother.

When Moselle pulled up to Shiloh's home, she was more than overwhelmed by the cars. She remembered him saying his family would be there but she hadn't expected anyone other that his parents and maybe a couple cousins. This looked a small family reunion.

She toyed with the idea of leaving and calling later feigning sickness. But she knew she'd be unable to look him in the face after that. So she found a place to park and walked up to his front door.

After she rang the door bell a couple of times to no avail, she realized there was soft music and voices coming from the backyard. A feeling of anxiety overcame her as she realized entering through the back would send her directly into the midst of a family she didn't know.

Moselle glanced down at the sundress she'd chosen to wear. It was deep red with small white Calla Lilies across the body. It was made of material that clung to her accentuating her curves. Because her feminine assets were more pronounced in her lower half than upper, she wasn't wearing a bra.

"What were you thinking, Mo?!" She said to herself, followed by, *"I am just so not used to this family thing."* Just as she turned to walk back to her car, she heard a voice.

"May I help you?"

She looked up to see a gentleman who looked a lot like Shiloh only shorter. "Yes, well, I'm a guest of, Shiloh. I'm here for Tristan's Birthday celebration."

"Oh, you must be his girlfriend. He's been looking for you. Come on; we're just about to start. I'm Boo-Boo by the way, Shi's first cousin."

"I thought we were having cake and ice cream." She followed closely behind Boo.

"And I thought you was from N'walins," Boo answered with a grin.

"Well, no my parents are. I was born and raised here in Richmond."

Boo-Boo stopped and regarded Mo for a second. "I guess your family's been gone so long they forgot."

"Forgot what?" Moselle felt a little defensive.

"Nothin's done small in *Louzianna*; we have a party for everything." And then he took her by the hand and said, "Come on baby girl; relax. You're gonna have a good time."

Chapter 14

Moselle had never seen so many people in one place at one time who called themselves family and got along. Although her parents still had relatives in Louisiana and along the east coast, they rarely got together.

To say she was overwhelmed was an understatement. The blessing was Shiloh, Ines or Boo-Boo was with her at all times. Shiloh made it his business to introduce her to each and everyone present. The only names she retained were Boo-Boo, Ines and Robert whom she referred to as Mr. and Mrs. Milner.

That was until Ines refused to answer her until she called her by her first name.

"No daughter-in-law of mine will be calling me Mrs. Milner or Mrs. Ines," she said to her husband sarcastically.

"What do you mean by that?" Robert said obviously defensive.

"Just help me put the rest of this food out Rob." With that, Ines walked out the door.

"How you know they gonna get married anyway," he said under his breath. "Get on my nerves with all that MoJo."

"I heard that!" Ines said and rolled her eyes.

With the festivities concluded and Tristan tucked in bed, Shiloh walked Moselle to her car. "You didn't have to drive ya know; I would have picked you up. Now you have to drive home alone and it's getting dark."

"I'll be okay. I'll call when I get there."

"How about I follow you," he said and pulled his keys from his pocket. He knew she had driven herself as a protective move. If she became too uncomfortable, she could leave whenever she wanted as opposed to having to wait on him.

"I'm fine baby, besides I'm stopping past Tangy's on the way home."

He frowned, "This time of night?"

"It's not that late, it's just that the days are getting shorter."

Shiloh narrowed his eyes. "Okay and how is that different from what I said."

"I'll be fine baby. Actually, if it will make you feel better, why don't you follow me to Tangy's and I'll get Max, her husband, to follow me home.

"Alright, let me tell my parents and I'll be right back."

Before they got into their cars to leave, Shiloh pulled Moselle to him and gave her a long passionate kiss. "Thank you for coming baby; I really appreciate it. Plus, I enjoyed showing you off."

"Ummm, it was my pleasure. By the way, I see where you get your cooking skills. I have to get my mom to teach me some of those recipes."

"I thought you said your mother didn't cook *Louzianna* style."

"She doesn't, but if I want you around, I'm going to have to get busy."

"Well if that doesn't pan out, I'm sure my mother would be more than happy to help you. Plus, she knows all my favorites.

"Seems like a nice young lady," Robert said to Shiloh once he returned home.

"So you like her huh?"

"Yes, actually I do. She told me her parents are from N'awlins but don't get down to visit very much. When I asked her why, she didn't seem to know or didn't say."

"I don't think they are as close a family as we are."

"Well, just make sure that's not a hindrance."

"How is that a hindrance Dad?"

"Shiloh, you know good and well how important family is to folk from *Louzianna;* something's up."

"I agree with family being important, but if her parents are estranged from their family members, that has nothing to do with Mo and me."

"I know it's early on but I'm going to give you a piece of advice. Remember when you marry her, you marry her family. Your mother would agree."

"Agree to what?" Ines said having heard her name.

"I was just telling Shiloh that I thought it strange Moselle's parents didn't return home much except for weddings and funerals."

"She did say that, but I'm sure there's a good reason," Ines said.

"Let it go dad. You are no longer in law enforcement. Stop being suspicious of everyone and everything, relax." Shiloh placed his hand on his father's shoulder as he spoke.

"He's right Rob. Now let's go home. I'm tired and I have to be back over here in the morning. Have you forgotten its Sunday?" Ines said.

"Nope, I haven't forgotten. Good night Son." Robert stood to his feet.

"Good night." Shiloh reached out and hugged first his father and then his mother. "Thank you for everything."

"Not a problem, you're our son." Ines answered.

After walking his family to the door and making sure all the doors and windows were locked, Shiloh went to check on Tristan. As he looked down at the sleeping baby he couldn't help but think of Angela.

"I know this wasn't the ideal way for Tristan to come into my life, but now that he's here I can't imagine myself without him. I pray for Angie wherever she is that she finds peace and . . . You. Because whatever it is she's looking for, it can only be found in You." He prayed.

He scooped his sleeping son up and kissed his face. Instead of placing him back into his crib, Shiloh carried him into his room and placed him in his bed.

Chapter 15

Tangy and Moselle settled into Tangy's overstuffed sofa and jumped right into conversation. "So, tell me about the party," Tangy said as she sipped on her tea. She had made the two of them a cup of chamomile tea.

"Girl, I haven't seen that many family members in one place in a long while. He's from a huge family."

"And does that scare you?"

"No, why should it scare me? I found it a little overwhelming but not scary."

Tangy lifted her cup to her lips and mumbled, "Ummm hummm."

"And what does that mean?" Mo asked primping her lips.

"Nothing, I'm just saying."

Moselle sat her cup down on the table beside her. "Tangy, we go way back; I know you. You meant something. Anyway, why do you always do that? Just say what you mean."

"Well, Stone came from a large family and I'm just wondering if you're going to be okay with that."

Moselle folded her arms across her chest. She took a minute before she spoke. "Stone was a liar and a cheat. He used any excuse he could to sleep around, including the play cousin thing."

"For your information Ms Thang," she continued, "I've worked through all that."

Tangy broke into a broad smile. She reached over and held Moselle's hand. "I'm so happy to hear that. I know you've said it before Mo, but this time I can tell you feel it - right here." She added touching the area over her heart.

"So, tell me all about your handsome man. 'Cause girl, he is fine. I know you been holdin' back on me this time . . . waiting to be sure," Tangy leaned into Mo as she said that piece, "But I want to know it all."

"Well, you know I still grapple with his job, but I'm working through that too."

Tangy frowned and gave Moselle a playful slap on the hand. "You better. Don't ever let a man's profession dictate whether or not you'll date him."

"I know, I know," Moselle said, "Stone made six figures and was a jerk."

"Yes, put a big 'ole concussion diamond on your hand and was a sleepin' around fool."

"What I appreciate most about Shiloh is he respects me. In the three months we've dated, he's never tried to get me in the bed. He's kept his hands to himself, even his kisses are respectful."

"Wow, Mo. This is what you've been praying for. Look at God. How are his parents? Are they as sweet as he is?"

"Yes they are. As a matter of fact, I met them for the first time today. They insisted I call them by their first names and treated me like family."

"Ummm hummm, not boo-gee huh?" Tangy took a sip of her tea with a look of sarcasm to match her statement.

"No, even though I can tell Ines and Robert love Shiloh, they don't worship him."

"Or expect everyone else too, huh?"

"Girl, you know you wrong," Mo said before bursting into a full belly laugh.

"Alright ladies," Maxwell, Tangy's husband said interrupting the women. "I gotta work in the morning. So if I'm following you home Moselle, we need to get moving."

Later that night after she settled into bed, Moselle phoned Shiloh to let him know she'd made it home safely. Although it was past midnight, they talked for two more hours. As always before he said goodnight, Shiloh prayed for Moselle.

When she hung up the phone, she pinched herself to make sure she wasn't dreaming. After all she'd endured at the hands of Stone, God had finally blessed her.

Chapter 16

Shiloh felt as though he hadn't slept in days. Tristan's crying seemed unending. "Mom!"

"Yesssss . . ." Ines answered from her bedroom in his home.

"You sure we don't need to take him to the emergency room?!"

Ines made her way into her son's room. She could tell by the expression on his face that he was panicking. He held his son close to his chest and frantically rocked the wailing baby.

"Shiloh, Tristan is fine. He just had his baby shots and the doctor told you he may be fussy and run a low-grade fever."

"I know Ma, but he's been crying for awhile and now he has loose bowels."

Ines took a deep breath. She knew Shiloh was doing his best but she was losing patience. "Baby, I won't tell you anything wrong. If we take the baby to the ER, they will only ask you when was the last time he had 'Tylenol' and give him some if they think he needs it."

Shiloh looked as if he was about to cry along with his son. "I just can't stand to see him like this."

"Sweetie, this is just the beginning. There will be many times when you will console your baby even after he's grown." She smiled and reached for her grandson.

"Take a nap; I'll rock him for awhile." She added.

Although Shiloh lay across his bed, he couldn't sleep. His mind was on his son and a part of him was angry with Angie for leaving him this way. On impulse, he reached for the phone and dialed Moselle.

Moselle glanced at the clock before she picked up her phone. She looked at the caller ID and then answered. "Shiloh, what's wrong baby?"

"Tristan got his shots today and he's been miserable. I wanted to take him to the ER but my mother thinks he'll be fine."

"What's he doing? Is he crying?"

"Yes, pretty much nonstop. But that's not why I called you. I called because I needed to hear your voice so I can relax and sleep."

"Shi, you know I don't mind coming over if you need me."

"No Mo. Like I said, that's not why I called you. I'm not taking advantage of your kindness."

"Its okay babe. I don't mind coming over if you want." Moselle sat up on the side of the bed. "I really don't. I can be there in less than 20 minutes," she added.

"Moselle, if I wanted you to come over I would ask. Really, I'm okay. I just have to get use to being a father. Mom's probably right anyway. The pediatrician and nurse told me Tristan would act this way."

"You sure?"

"Completely. I just needed to hear your voice baby. I feel so much better. As a matter of fact, I think I'm going to take that nap my mother suggested."

"Okay baby. But before you go, let me pray for you and Tristan the way you always pray for me."

Chapter 17

"So, how are things going with that handsome man of yours?" Tangy asked. She and Moselle were having lunch at their favorite eatery, *Ty's Internet Café and lounge.*

"Actually, things are good." Mo paused. "You know what I love about him most?"

"You betta tell it," Tangy said.

There is no pressure for sex."

Tangy almost spit her drink out at Moselle's comment. "When did you start feeling that way Ms. Thang? You usually enjoy intimacy with your boo."

"I sure do but Shiloh wants to wait until marriage and I like the idea of that. It's sweet and what God wants for us."

Tangy smiled. "You are so right and I will be praying for you that you and Shiloh succeed. I wish Max and I could have done that but as the Bible says, 'The spirit is willing but the flesh is weak.'"

"Well pray me through Sis, 'cause I know it's not going to be easy, but we're determined."

Just as the words left Moselle's lips her cell phone rang. She glanced at the caller ID, with the expectation of seeing Shiloh's name. When her smile turned into a frown, Tangy knew something was wrong.

"What's up?" She asked her friend.

"I can't believe this! After all this time!" Mo looked at Tangy; the disdain was evident on her face.

"Moselle, who is it?"

The phone stopped ringing, and shortly after the musical sound indicated a voice mail had been left chimed. "Do you remember Majid?"

"Majid? Of course, who could forget him?" Mumbling under her breath, Tangy added, "With his fine self."

"Tangy! Focus!" Moselle yelled. "Majid was a stone cold trip." She sat back and folded her arms across her chest.

"Yeah, but he was a fine trip and you said his lips were like lethal weapons."

Moselle sighed and her facial expression relaxed a bit. "Yeah, he could kiss . . . but."

"But you are exactly right. I'm just getting caught up," Tangy said. "That probably ain't nothin' but the devil showing up to mess you up since you and Shi are doing so well."

Moselle nodded her head in agreement.

Tangy glanced at her watch, "I gotta run babe; let me know what home-slice says." After she stood, she looked at Moselle and added, "All jokes aside, be careful Mo. I meant what I said about the devil."

"I will," Moselle added as she gave her girlfriend a hug.

Something about the way Tangy's warning sounded bothered her but she shrugged it off. *"I love my man, ain't nothin' Majid can do for me,"* she said to herself.

She gathered her purse and headed out the door after she paid the check. Seated behind the wheel of her car, Moselle stared at the icon that meant she had a voice message. Against her better judgment, she listened to it.

Majid, had left his phone number with a request she return his call. She took a deep breath and hit the redial button although deep inside she knew she should run for the nearest exit.

Chapter 18

Majid answered on the second ring. "Hey gorgeous, I was hoping against hope you'd call."

"Oh really . . . how are you Majid?" Moselle's tone was so flat it caused him to wince.

"I've been good . . . but as the old cliché goes, 'I'm better now that I'm talking with you.'"

Mo rolled her eyes and willed herself not to give him her forgiveness that easily.

"You there Zell?" He used his nickname for her.

"I'm here. So, what's up?

"Wow baby, why you say it like that?"

"You know? I used to think you'd lost your mind. Now I'm convinced."

"Zell, why are you coming at me like that? We haven't talked in a year and a half and you beatin' me up with your words out the gate."

Moselle shook her head and then took a deep breath. She knew she was falling right back into the same old pattern with Majid. Before she opened her eyes, she willed herself to be strong.

"Why the call Majid, as you just said we haven't talked in over a year." This time her tone was a little more accepting.

"I've missed you, that's all." Majid paused, "I just want to talk."

"About?"

"About what happened between us, Zell. I owe you an apology."

"You owe me a lot more than that," Moselle snapped.

"Okay, I'll give you that one . . . Look, may we meet somewhere? I don't want to do this over the phone."

"No."

Majid pulled the phone away from his ear and looked at it. "No?" He repeated in disbelief.

"That's right, I said no. Whatever you have to say, say it to me on the phone."

"Look," he pushed ahead, not willing to give up that easily. "I just want to see you for a few minutes. I'm tryin' to give you a proper apology." His voice softened, "You deserve that much Zell."

Moselle felt that part of her known for the flight or fight kick in. With everything in her, she knew she should refuse his offer. But the piece of him still living within her heart wouldn't let her. Deep inside she realized there was still a love for him she'd yet to get over.

"I don't know. I'm seeing someone now and he's a good man." Her voice dropped to a whisper, but he knew it was much more.

Majid knew her well enough to know those words were a plea to be left alone. But he refused to let it be. "It's just drinks; I just want to take you for drinks. I want to apologize to you face to face. Maybe salvage what friendship we have left."

"We don't have a friendship. You blew that."

"Okay, well then let me buy you dinner and a drink, apologize, and I promise I won't bother you again."

"When and where would you like to meet?" Moselle's inner warning kicked up a notch, but she pushed the feeling down.

Chapter 19

Three hours later Moselle pulled into the parking lot of a restaurant in the Fredericksburg area of Virginia. Approximately 75 miles north of her Chesterfield County home. She'd rushed home after work, showered and changed prior to meeting him.

Looking down at herself, she took inventory of her outfit. The September weather was just cool enough in the evenings for her to get away with straight-leg jeans. She'd worn a black pair that fit more like a glove than pants - highlighting her shapely legs and curvy derriere. The cascading neckline of her Persian Green top draped just low enough on her chest to entice but leave what lie behind it to the imagination.

As she reached for her purse, Shiloh's smile came to mind. Moselle pushed the image aside, swallowed her guilt and climbed from the car.

She was relieved Majid had chosen an eatery in the area where he was staying instead of the Metro Richmond area. This way she didn't risk running into anyone who knew her or Shiloh. Taking a deep breath, she entered the establishment and approached the hostess.

"Good evening, welcome to Luis' Place. Just one in your party tonight?" The hostess greeted Moselle with a smile.

"Ummm, no I'm meeting someone." Mo stammered in response.

"Ah, yes. You must be Ms. Laveau, Mr. Mason's guest," she said glancing down at her reservation sheet. "He's right this way."

The hostess turned on her heels and led Moselle into the room. Majid smiled and rose to his feet when he saw them approaching. The sight of him still took her breath away.

He leaned into her and kissed her cheek. His lips lingered just a little longer than they probably should have. In his mind, this was the way it always went between them after a fight. Tonight was no different for him.

"Wow babe. You look great," Majid said as he pulled Moselle's chair out for her.

"Your server will be right with you to take Ms. Laveau's drink order," the hostess said as she headed back to her post.

Majid reached out and took Mo's hand. "It's good to see you Zell."

"Thanks," she mumbled as she pulled her hand away. "It's good to see you too. I see you are as put together as ever," Moselle said with a smile.

"It's good to see you finally smile," he added with a grin.

Moselle caught herself getting lost in his dark eyes - those eyes that pierced her to her core. They spoke of his Middle Eastern heritage as did his name.

"So, you wanted to talk?" she said as she glanced at her watch feigning indifference.

"Are you in a hurry?"

"Yes, sort of. It's late and I have to travel back to Chesterfield alone."

"Moselle, it's only eight o'clock on a Friday night. Can't you hang out with an old friend for a couple hours?"

"Okay, I'll give you until ten because I don't want to be on the road much after then by myself."

Majid smiled. He knew her well enough to know she was playing hard. But then again, why shouldn't she, he'd messed up.

Just as he opened his mouth to speak, the server showed up to take Moselle's drink order. When she ordered a soft drink, he talked her into having a glass of wine. "One Zell. Just one."

The Jazz band for the evening took the stage shortly after her drink was served and they'd ordered dinner. Moselle was thankful for the distraction, however brief. It gave her a chance to pull herself together.

Moselle methodically ate her meal. Although Majid had suggested the best entrée on the menu, she barely tasted the food. Her mind kept drifting back to Shiloh and what they were building. As quickly as thoughts of him surfaced, she pushed them down.

After only finishing half of her meal, she told Majid she was full. "Do you want me to have it wrapped?"

"Sure, that would be nice," she answered. When the band took a brief intermission, Mo took that as an opportunity to excuse herself to the women's room.

Raising Tristan

"What the heck are you doing?" She asked herself while she washed her hands. Her reflection stared back at her. Frown lines formed across her forehead and her eyes appeared weary.

"I am not that weak for this man, not anymore. I'm much stronger than this." Grabbing her purse and steeling her shoulders, Moselle headed back to the table to retrieve her leftovers and head home.

"Majid, I'm calling it a night. I've got an hour and a half drive ahead of me," she said as she reached for the boxed food.

As she turned to walk away, Majid grabbed her arm. "Dance with me Zell, please. Just one dance before you go."

The band began to play *"Why Would You Stay,"* by *Kem*. The piano player took the microphone and sang almost as sweetly as *Kem* himself.

Moselle felt herself being led to the dance floor and she was powerless to stop herself. Majid sang softly into her ear as he held her close. She'd forgotten how well he sang - how his words set to song never failed to melt her.

Halfway through the rendition, he planted a soft kiss on her neck and whispered, "forgive me baby" into her collarbone.

Moselle knew exactly how things would play out. She knew exactly what came next. This is the way it always was. He'd hurt her; disappear for awhile and come back begging.

His kisses soft on her neck would leave her powerless; his words would leave her wet with desire. Her heart would open up and she'd take him back hoping against hope that this would be the last time he broke her heart. But it never was.

This time was different. She had the ammunition she needed to resist him. She had Shiloh, a man who loved her with all his being. She had a man who respected her and God enough to wait until marriage to make love to her. This time she told herself she could turn and walk away and never look back.

Chapter 20

When Majid's lips grazed Moselle's ankle, she repeated Shiloh's name in her head. When his hand stroked her hip, she attempted to say her love's name aloud. When his hardness found her center, she raised her pelvis to meet him and allowed the tears she was holding to cascade from her eyes.

Majid's love making was sweeter than Mo remembered. His mouth was like fire on her skin and she knew she was in danger. His kisses were crack-cocaine to her. Try though she may, she never could resist them.

With each of his strokes, she found herself farther and farther away from Shiloh and the safety of his arms. Finally in an effort to erase the guilt building in her gut, she blocked him out completely.

Her body trembled in response to Majid's touch over and over. Each time she felt she could not orgasm again; he sent her spinning into ecstasy once more.

When their bodies were finally spent and exhausted, he held her close as she silently wept. He promised Moselle things would be different this time.

Majid told her he'd learned his lesson and would never betray her trust again. He explained he'd come to realize she was his soul mate - the woman he wanted to marry and spend the rest of his life with.

"I want you to be my wife, Zell. I want you to have my babies." Moselle didn't answer. For the first time in her life, she was confused. She just layed in his arms and cried.

"Who's at the door this time of night, Tangy?" Max asked a bit irritated that his rest was broken.

"How should I know?" She sounded equally as annoyed.

Raising Tristan

Maxwell turned on the lamp and glanced at the clock. It was three o'clock in the morning. "The last time somebody knocked on my door at this hour it was to tell me my dad was gone. This better be equally as important," he said as he slipped on his pajama bottoms.

Tangy grabbed her caftan and slid it over her head. She knew her husband had a temper, and if it was one of his buddy's who happened to stop by in a drunken stupor, she knew she'd have to intervene.

"Coming, keep you draws on!" Max's voice boomed through the house as the doorbell rang for the second time.

"Max, keep it down before you wake up the kids," Tangy admonished.

When he opened the door, his expression went from one of irritation to alarm. "Mo, what the . . . what are you doing here this time of night?"

Tangy reached around him and pulled Moselle into the fourier. Moselle fell into her arms and began to weep.

"Let's get her into the kitchen before the children hear her and come down," Maxwell said.

As Moselle sat and cried, Max and Tangy exchanged glances. To say a usually put together Mo looked disheveled was an understatement.

Her hair had the appearance of someone who'd just awakened from a deep sleep and her clothes seemed to be thrown on hurriedly.

They sat on either side of her and waited until she was composed enough to talk. "What's wrong Mo?" Tangy asked.

"Did someone hurt you?" Maxwell asked. He didn't verbalize it, but to him, Moselle had the appearance of a woman who'd been raped.

"No," Moselle replied softly. She blew her nose into the napkins Tangy handed her.

After a few minutes Max asked again, "Well, what is it? What's wrong?"

"Can I just talk with Tangy by herself?" Mo answered through her sniffles.

Maxwell leaned back in his chair and crossed his arms. "Moselle, you may be Tangy's best friend but it's obvious someone has done something awful to you. Now, if you were raped—"

"I wasn't raped! Please, just let me talk to Tangy."

"Moselle, listen to me. You come knocking on my door at three o'clock in the morning looking like you were attacked or something and crying hysterically . . . Now, I'm not moving until you tell me and Tangy what's up. I owe Shiloh that. Because if it were Tangy, I know he'd do the same for me."

Moselle began to cry harder. "Did Shiloh do something to you?" Max asked. He sat forward and placed his hand on Mo's shoulder.

"No! Shiloh would never hurt me!"

"Then what is it sweetie?" Tangy asked softly.

Moselle took a deep breath and blurted out, "I was with another man!"

"I was with Majid . . ." she added as she reached for Tangy. "I slept with him T, what am I going to do?"

As if on queue, Maxwell looked at is wife, nodded and left the room.

Moselle blew her nose again. "I can't believe I fell for him that easily Tangy. What is wrong with me?"

"There is nothing wrong with you Mo."

"Well, then why can't I ever say no to him? Why is it that Majid can disappear out of my life for an entire year and I just fall into his trap?"

"You're still in love with him."

Moselle's tears suddenly turned to sniffles. She looked at Tangy as if she'd seen a ghost. When she found her voice, she mumbled, "No, I'm not."

"Yes, you are sweetie. The sooner you accept that, the sooner you can move on and really give Shiloh your heart."

The next few minutes felt like an hour to Moselle as she grappled to understand what her friend was saying to her. As far as she was concerned, she had given her heart to Shiloh. She was even ready to be his wife should he ask. How could her best friend think otherwise?

She shook her head from side to side and again denied what Tangy had said. "I don't love Majid, not anymore."

"Well then, why did you allow him to pull you into this mess with him again?" Tangy leaned forward and took Mo's hands into hers.

"Mo, there are some men whom we will love for a lifetime. It doesn't make us bad women, just human. The problem comes when we don't acknowledge that piece so we can be free."

"But, I really don't love him . . ."

"Okay, maybe you don't. Maybe I'm totally off base. Anyway, the thing now is, where do you go from here? Majid is not going to quietly go away."

"I know . . . what am I going to do?"

"If you don't love him, you're going to call him up and tell him. And you're going to tell him to stay away from you."

Moselle turned and looked out the kitchen window. Tangy knew her well enough to know Mo's lack of response meant trouble.

"Moselle, you aren't going to continue this, are you? You know a relationship with Majid always leads to nowhere."

Silence followed her question. "Mo? Moselle!"

"Yes! I heard you Tangy. Look I know Shiloh is a good man and I know beyond a shadow of doubt he loves me."

"Well, then, what is the problem?"

"I don't know. I guess old feelings just die hard." Hanging her head, she added, "Even though I didn't speak on it much, I always wished things had worked out between Majid and me."

"You didn't have to speak on it; I know you Mo. But history between you and Majid . . . Well, it's always the same ending."

"Don't throw away what you're building with a man who knows what he wants for someone who comes running back to you when he realizes what he thought was a better relationship turns out to be something different." Tangy added.

"I know," Moselle replied.

"Look," Tangy started, "it's late and we're both tired. The boys will be up in a little while looking for their Saturday morning full breakfast, so why don't you lie down in the guest room."

"No, I think I'm going home. I need to be in my own bed tonight," Moselle answered.

Just as she finished, her cell phone buzzed. Glancing at the caller ID, she saw it was Majid. When she looked at Tangy, her face said it all.

"Answer it. Maybe he's calling to see if you made it home safely." Tangy's voice dripped with sarcasm. It was obvious Majid was not one of her favorite people.

"Hello?"

"Hey, baby. I hadn't heard from you, just checkin' to make sure you made it home okay." Majid said.

"Ummm, yeah, I'm good."

"Cool. Call me when you get up. I'll come down and take you to brunch."

"Okay, that sounds nice," Moselle hoped her tone didn't give her away, but Tangy was all over it. She knew her best friend well enough to know it was going to take a trip around that same mountain to prove to her Majid would never be the man he claimed he was. Not now, not ever.

Tangy silently prayed God would protect Moselle's heart and shield her relationship with Shiloh. "My friend is making a terrible mistake, God, please be with her."

Moselle disconnected her call and gave Tangy a sheepish look. "He was wondering if I made it, just like you said."

'Why didn't you tell him I said hi?" Tangy said with the disdain she felt for Majid written all over her face.

Gathering her things, Moselle said, "I'm not going to do anything else foolish; you don't have to worry."

"Okay." Tangy pulled Moselle into a brief hug and then walked her to the door. "Call when you get home and don't forget."

"I won't. Love you girl."

"I love you more," Tangy said as she watched her friend walk to her car.

"Well, I can have some of my boys give him a beat-down," Max said.

"How long have you been standing there?" Tangy asked with a chuckle.

"Long enough babes. Long enough."

Chapter 21

"Good morning beautiful." Shiloh's voice pulled Moselle from her sleep. It seemed she had just drifted off when her phone rang. A glance at the clock proved her feelings to be correct. She had indeed only been asleep for four hours.

"I was calling to see if you'll be meeting Tristan and me at church or if you want me to pick you up." He continued.

"Ummm, good morning to you too, babe." She hoped the guilt that suddenly rose up and choked her wasn't evident in her voice. "It seems I've overslept; so I'll meet you there."

"Okay, we'll be sitting in our usual area. Oh, and by the way, Mom and Dad want Tristan for this afternoon. After church he's going with them."

"Something special going on?"

"Yes, they figured out you don't have call today, and thought we'd enjoy some time."

Majid's offer for brunch suddenly came across Moselle's mind. Her hands started to tremble and she struggled to keep her tone even. "That's sweet baby."

"I thought we'd have a picnic and then take in a movie. How does that sound?"

"Well, I don't know."

Shiloh frowned, "What do you mean you don't know? How often do we get time alone? I thought you'd jump at the opportunity."

Mo felt the flesh on her inner thighs quiver at the memory of Majid's lips touching her there. She knew the right thing to do was to spend the day with Shiloh, but her body had a mind of its own and it craved more.

"Are you there, Mo? Is everything okay?"

Moselle took a deep breath and shook her head. "Yes. I'm here Shiloh; I'm just a little tired. I'd love to spend the day with you baby. Now, I better hang up and get myself ready for church."

"Cool, see you in a few."

Just as she disconnected her call from Shiloh, her phone buzzed again; this time it was Majid. "Hey Zell, I thought you were going to call me when you got up."

"I haven't been up very long, what's up?" Moselle's guilty conscious kicked into overdrive.

"Well, I'd planned on taking you to brunch, remember?"

"Majid," she started, "I can't. I have church and then…"

"Okay, I see, you got something with this guy you're seeing, right?" He chuckled.

"Last night never should have happened, Majid."

"But it did, Moselle. And if this guy you're seeing was all that, you wouldn't have found yourself in my bed."

"Everybody makes mistakes sometimes, and last night was a mistake."

Majid chuckled again, "A mistake huh? Yeah, right. The only mistake was me letting you get away, but I'm going to fix that. This ain't over, Zell. I'm not walking away that easily."

"I have to go Majid. I need to get ready for church."

"Alright, may I call you later?"

Moselle knew that answer should have been no, but instead, she quietly replied, "I'll call you."

Chapter 22

Shiloh picked up on the change in Moselle's behavior immediately. But he wasn't the only one who sensed a change, so did Ines. For once, she prayed her instincts were wrong.

All throughout the service, Moselle seemed preoccupied and indeed she was. Her mind kept drifting back to Saturday night and Majid's hands in places that should have been reserved for her boyfriend alone.

After church she asked Shiloh to meet her at her home so that she could change into something more suitable for a picnic. Her true reason for the alone time was to call Majid and make sure she didn't hear from him until *she* called him later that night.

"That's cool," he said, "But I still want to see you, Zell. I need to see you tonight, please."

As if by clock work, the flesh on her inner thigh quivered again and the need to feel his hands on her took over. "Okay, but just for tonight and just to talk; I mean it."

"I'll take what I can get. Call me when you get in and I'll head down." Majid smiled to himself as he hung up the phone. Things were turning out just as he'd planned. Soon he'd have Moselle back at his side where she belonged, and this time he'd make sure she stayed.

He flipped open the blue velvet box on his night stand. The 5.0 carat solitaire diamond shimmered in the light. *"I know I've messed up big time in the past Zell, but I've changed and I'm going to show you, not tell you. Because I know you well enough to know that's what it's going to take,"* He said to himself.

After he closed the box and placed it in his hotel room safe, he picked up the business card to the best realtor in the area and dialed her number.

He would need a nice home in the Prince George County area of Maryland, one large enough to hold the family he planned on starting with Moselle.

Knowing her the way he did, she would want to work outside the home at least a few days a week. He figured the area would be perfect. Moselle could work in private practice with a local Pediatrician and still have time for a family.

He may have been a lot of undesirable things when it came to being her love but the one thing he was good at was business. Majid had made money investing and reinvesting during their time apart.

Things had gone so well for him during that year and a half that he had substantially added to his already padded portfolio in spite the economy.

Majid was doing well when he was with Moselle which was a part of his problem. He had used his money to woo women, even if they were the wrong women. But regardless, his Broker was a shrewd investor and with his advice, he had put Majid into the Millionaire status.

He knew he had to come back a better man in order to win her back. He figured she would be involved with someone. He just never imagined it would be serious.

"That's fine," He said to himself, *"I know you baby-girl. I know how you like your love making and I know how you like to live."*

"Not only am I going to make mind blowing love to you every chance I get, I'm going to set you up in a half-million dollar home that will make your mouth water."

With that, Majid dialed the number on the card and made an appointment for the following Tuesday to begin looking at houses.

Chapter 23

Moselle's silence began to make Shiloh uncomfortable to the point he pulled the car over into a random shopping center. He turned to her determined to find out why the abrupt change in her behavior.

"So, what's up babe; why do you seem so distant all of a sudden? You're not yourself."

The tension in the air rose as Mo struggled to come up with an answer. "It's my job, baby. We've all been stressed out lately. Our census is high and the babies are real sick." She turned to him.

"I apologize for bringing this into our relationship."

Shiloh cupped her face in his hands and pulled her to him. He planted a kiss on her forehead. "You don't have to apologize, babe, I understand. But you know you can talk to me about anything, right?"

Moselle nodded. "Well, if you ever want to talk about your job and what goes on, I'm here for you." He finished and then gently kissed her lips.

She leaned into her love and reminded herself of how sweet he was. She reminded herself of the bright future she knew she would have with him, instead of the dead-end street she was headed down with Majid.

"Now, let's go eat some of this delicious food I picked up for us."

Moselle turned her face and gazed out the window. As she watched the scenery pass by, she heard her grandmother's voice whisper in her head. *"Don't ever tell a lie baby, 'cause if you do, you got to continue to lie to cover up that first lie."*

"I know Gramy . . . I know . . . I'm going to tell Majid that it's over tonight. And then I'm going stay away from him for good because I don't ever want to lie to Shiloh again." She said to herself.

"How was the picnic?" Ines asked Shiloh when he returned home.

"It was good . . . Mo's having a hard time at work, so we talked about that."

"How's she having a rough time of it; she seems like she's pretty good at her job."

"Well, it's not that, there are a lot of sick children and she's feeling pretty drained."

Ines paused. She knew there was more to the story, but she also knew it was not her place to say anything about what she was feeling. Her son would have to find out on his own.

"Your son is fast asleep," his mother said, changing the subject. "I'm going to head home; your father and I have a few things to do around the house before we turn in."

"Thanks Mom," Shiloh said, as he kissed his mother goodnight. "I think I'm going to take a shower and call Moselle. I know we just left one another but I like lying in bed and talking to her."

Ines smiled, "I remember feeling that way about your father when we were young. You have a good night baby."

"Thanks Mom. I love you and tell Dad goodnight. I love him, too."

Shiloh walked his mother to her car and gave her another hug and kiss before she pulled off. He headed back inside and checked on Tristan before he took a shower.

Once the water began to hit his back and he stated to relax, he thought about his mother's reaction to the explanation for Moselle's behavior. Shiloh knew his mother well, and he knew her reaction was weighted. But he also knew that whatever was bothering her would remain with her. He just hoped that whatever it was wouldn't turn out to his nightmare.

Chapter 24

Majid buzzed the doorbell to Moselle's a little after midnight. He'd intentionally arrived this late. He knew she'd be showered and in her pajamas. His plan was to stay the night and her being half dressed was half his battle.

The doorbell startled her as she had just dozed off to sleep. When Moselle glanced at the clock, she wondered who could be at her door this late. She knew it couldn't be Tangy unless something was dreadfully wrong.

As she made her way to the door, a feeling of dread filled her stomach and she released the safety on her nine millimeter gun, a gift from her father, Sean Laveau when she moved away from home. He'd had taken her to a shooting range and insisted she learn to protect herself. *"You never know when you may run into a nut and have to defend yourself until the police arrive."*

Moselle held the gun close to her chest the way she'd been instructed and peered through the peep hole. When she saw it was Majid, her feeling of dread turned to anger.

"What are you doing here?!" she shouted. She kept her body between him and the entrance to her home.

"Well, damn baby, what were you planning to do, shoot me?" Majid asked, as he looked from the gun in her hand to her face.

"I should have."

"You don't mean that."

Moselle's frown deepened, "I asked what you're doing here Majid. I have to work tomorrow and my day starts early."

"I thought I was coming to spend some time the way we discussed." He answered with a smile beginning to form on his lips.

"If my memory serves me correct, *we* decided to make it another day. You said you were okay with that." Moselle was a bit put out by his grin.

"Can't I change my mind baby?" Majid moved close to her and placed his hands on her sides. He gently turned her so that he could step inside the foyer.

"You know what - I don't appreciate this at all. I told you I'm seriously dating and we could meet for coffee *only*, but not today."

Majid took the gun from her hand and placed it on a table near the door. He moved closer and planted a kiss on her cheek. Moselle felt her resolve begin to weaken, so she took a deep breath and squared her shoulders.

"I said no, Majid. I'm not interested."

"Okay," he responded as he planted another kiss on her forehead. "But just so you know, this time, I'm serious about us . . ."

He reached into his jacket pocket and pulled out a small velvet box and placed it in her hand.

Moselle looked at him with a puzzled look on her face. "What is this?"

"Open it."

Instead of following his request, she turned and headed into her den. After she had sat down on her sofa and Majid sat beside her, she the opened the box. The 5.0 carat Canary diamond caused her to gasp.

"What are you doing?" she asked in disbelief, "I haven't seen you in a year and a half and you think you can just walk back into my life and ask me to marry you?"

"What is wrong with you, Majid? Have you lost your mind?" She finished.

This time Majid took a deep breath. "No, I haven't lost my mind; if anything I've found it."

"Look Moselle," he continued, "I know I was a jerk when we were together. I broke your heart so many times; I'm surprised you even talk to me. But I learned something during that year and a half we were apart about me."

Before she could open her mouth to respond, he asked her to allow him to finish. "You are the best thing that ever happened to me and I swear to you if you give me a chance I'll prove it."

"I've hired a realtor in the Prince George County Maryland area, and I've started looking for a home for us. In the meantime, I've found a townhouse to move into so, I can be close to you."

"In Richmond?" Moselle asked with a look of shock on her face.

"No, in Prince George. I figured you'd need your space and I didn't want to crowd you."

"Majid, I don't know what to say to you," Moselle said as she shook her head. "Why are you doing this?"

"Because deep down on the inside of you, I know you still have some type of love for me, which I believe can be rekindled."

He put his finger against her lips when he saw she was about to speak. "And I know you have a new love, but he doesn't know you like I do."

"He doesn't know how you like to be kissed; he doesn't know how you like to be loved. He doesn't know that when you get too tired, your left eye turns in a little because you were born with a weak left eye muscle."

"Your boyfriend doesn't know that your favorite ice cream is really butter almond but you eat vanilla because butter almond is hard to find."

Moselle felt her eyes begin to tear up. "But he can learn all those things, Majid. He's a good man and he loves me. And more importantly, I love him."

Majid threw up both of his hands in a sign of surrender. "You're right . . . I'm not asking you to stop seeing him. All I'm asking for is a chance. That's all."

He pulled her to him and tenderly kissed her lips. "Just a half a chance and I promise you, you'll see I'm for real this time."

His hands found their way beneath her robe and stroked her body.

"No Majid, I did that once. I'm not cheating on Shiloh again." Moselle said. She pushed his hands away.

"Shiloh huh?" He said with a chuckle. "Okay, but does Shiloh know where your favorite spots are?"

Moselle felt her need take over when he touched her leg. She didn't want to be so weak but it had been a while since a man touched her in the way Majid did.

"I just want to please you before I go," he whispered into her ear.

After her body shuddered in release from his fingers, he simply kissed her good night and showed himself to the door.

Chapter 25

"It's hard to believe we've been together almost a year now," Shiloh said to Moselle. They were watching television at his home while Tristan was fast asleep. It was Moselle's weekend off.

"I know," she said. Her lips found their way to his and she gave him a quick kiss. "It feels longer, like I've known you a lifetime."

Shiloh's expression grew serious and he paused before he continued. "Sometimes it seems like you're so far away though Mo, like you aren't fully here anymore."

"What do you mean baby? Of course, I'm here with you. I love you." Moselle sat forward and turned to him.

"I don't doubt that you love me . . . It's just that sometimes it's almost like there's someone else."

Moselle leaned her forehead against Shiloh's and closed her eyes. "I love you baby, don't ever doubt that." She whispered.

Shiloh placed his hands on the sides of her head and lifted her face until her eyes met his. "I love you too - very much. I just want you to be sure this is where you want to be. After all, I'm a packaged deal."

Mo's head found its way to Shiloh's shoulder, and she snuggled under him and turned her attention to the movie. She slipped her hand into his and squeezed it. "I like packages."

She knew deep inside her answer didn't satisfy him, but it was the best one she had for the time.

"Tangy, I need to talk with you. Are you free for dinner?" Moselle asked her best friend a couple of days after her date with Shiloh.

"Sure, I'll let Max know we're hanging out; what's up?"

"I have something to show you."

"Okay, where do you want to meet?"

"Can you come over here? I'll cook."

"That's cool; I'll bring the wine."

Later that night Moselle and Tangy sat on her sun porch sipping on a glass of wine and having dessert. "So, what do you have to show me?" Tangy asked between bites of her cheesecake.

"Just a minute," Moselle said. She jumped up and dashed upstairs. She returned with a small velvet box which she handed to Tangy.

"Girl, what's this?" Tangy looked from the box to Moselle. Did Shiloh propose?"

Moselle shook her head. Tangy frowned and paused before opening the box. "Okay, if Shiloh didn't propose, what is this? Did you treat yourself to something nice?"

Again, Moselle shook her head. And this time, she seemed to grow nervous. "Just open it Tangy," she said.

Slowly Tangy did as she was told. When the box was completely opened, her chin almost hit her chest as her mouth flew open in surprise.

The 5.0 carat Canary Solitaire cut diamond surrounded by smaller white diamonds, took her breath away. Her hand flew to her chest as if trying to keep her heart in her chest.

"Moselle," Tangy said breathlessly, "where did you get this?"

"Majid—" Moselle started before Tangy cut her off.

"Majid! . . . Majid!! What is he doing giving you something like this? And what are you doing taking it?"

Taking a picture from the coffee table, she handed it to Tangy. "That's not all," she said as she shoved the picture into her friend's hand.

"Okay, Mo, you need to explain yourself right now." Tangy said as she glanced at the photograph of a beautiful two story, two car garage, and brick home.

Moselle took a deep breath before speaking. A few months ago Majid came by and brought me that ring. He said he was looking for a home in the Prince George County Maryland area for us. He said he wanted to marry me and spend the rest of his life with me."

"So, let me get this right," Tangy started, "You're having an affair with Majid." Her expression was one of disgust.

"Well, no . . . I'm so confused Tangy. Majid has been back in my life for more than six months and he has done everything he said he would. From the house to the ring to giving me time and space to think."

"Are you sleeping with him?"

Moselle grew silent.

"I said are you sleepin' with him Mo? And don't play with me, ' I know you."

"Oh Tangy, what am I going to do?' Moselle said before bursting into tears.

"Moselle, you've got to put a stop to this madness, Shiloh is a good man and he loves you. He doesn't deserve this."

"I know, but Majid has proven himself to me and he can give me the things I want and need."

"Is that what this is about, Mo? Money? Because if it is, I don't even know you right now." Tangy blurted out.

"How could you allow yourself to be drawn in by this foolishness? I mean, don't get me wrong, this ring is beautiful and this house is gorgeous. But I thought you were stronger than this?" Tangy shook her head in disbelief at her friend.

"I am. I know Shiloh is a good man and he loves me with all his heart. Tristan has become like my own son, but . . ."

"But what?"

"I don't know, Tangy. Maybe it's the way I was raised."

"Do not tell me you are hung up on that marrying up thing, Mo."

"It hangs in the back of my mind, Tangy. No matter how I try to shake it, I can't."

"Okay, see this is why your family is so damn boogie and don't get along."

"Oh, come on Tangy."

"You know I'm telling the truth. You've spent half your life trying to please your family and everybody else for that matter. When are you going to please Mo?"

Moselle continued to cry.

"Is it the sex Moselle? 'Cause I'm tryin' to figure out what you see in Majid."

"Thanks Tangy," Moselle squeaked out. "He's not that bad. As a matter of fact, he's changed."

"Changed?"

"Yes. He's done everything he swore he'd do. He's a better man now."

Tangy paused. "Well then, let Shiloh go Mo. Be honest with him and let him go."

Moselle's silence told Tangy she really was confused.

"Listen to me Mo. You're not only seeing Majid, you're sleeping with him. You have to be honest with Shiloh. If you don't want him, give him an opportunity to find someone who does."

Chapter 26

"Ohhhh Mo baby, you feel so good." Majid whispered in her ear. His hands gripped her pelvis pulling her closer to him as his release tore through him.

Tears of guilt trickled from Moselle's eyes in spite of the feeling of ecstasy that washed over her. She had not experienced many lovers but Majid was by far the best.

"What's wrong baby?" he asked noticing her tears.

"Nothing, I'm good."

"You sure? Is it me, didn't I please you?"

"It's nothing Majid . . . I just have a lot on my mind."

"Well, that's not good. I thought I took care of that. You should be super relaxed," he said and kissed her forehead.

Just as Majid pulled her to him, they heard what sounded like a key in the front door. Moselle sat straight up in bed. Her stomach tightened with anxiety and she instinctively grabbed for Majid.

"Oh no," she mumbled.

"Mo, what the hell is going on?" Majid asked as he sat up as well. "Is that who I think it is?"

When she didn't answer, Majid grabbed her face and turned it toward him. "I said is that who I think it is?" he repeated.

The look in her eyes was all the answer he needed. "You told me he was away for the day and wouldn't be around."

"I'm sorry; I thought he was out of town until tomorrow." She scrambled to untangle herself from the bed sheet.

Majid threw the linens from his body and stood to his feet as Moselle jumped out of bed and snatched her robe from the chaise in her bedroom.

The look on Majid's face told her she was in trouble. "Please stay here," she pleaded as she threw her robe about her and half ran half stumbled down the stairs.

Raising Tristan

Shiloh took one look at her disheveled appearance and automatically knew something was wrong. When the smell of raw sex oozing from her body hit his nose, his fears were confirmed.

His first impulse was to grab and shake her and ask her why, but he caught himself. He was so enraged. He knew that if he touched her he would hurt her. And so, instead he just glared at her.

The tears came bursting from Moselle's eyes like a flood. "I'm so sorry Shi, baby. I'm so sorry," she repeated over and over as she wrapped her arms around herself in an effort to hide her nakedness.

When Shiloh finally found his voice, it sounded totally unfamiliar to even him. "Are you cheatin' on me Moselle. You screwin' another man?!"

Moselle's tears kicked up another notch. "Answer me, Moselle. 'Cause it's everything I got in me right now not to beat the shit outta you."

Still she remained silent; her hands covered her face as she wept.

"Answer me damn it!"

"Yes . . ." Her words were barely above a whisper.

Just as the words left her lips, Shiloh heard footsteps above his head. "Awww hell naw," he said as he pushed past her and took the steps two at a time.

Moselle turned and ran behind him. "Shiloh, wait! Please wait!"

Majid and Shiloh stood face to face. The smell of his woman's body scent emanating from Majid's skin further infuriated Shiloh. When Moselle entered the room, he spoke to her in a low and menacing tone but his eyes never left Majid's.

"Is this where you wanna be, Moselle?"

The sound of the two men breathing was the only thing Moselle heard. She stood frozen to the floor. In her heart of hearts she knew belonged with Shiloh, but the future promised by Majid hung in her mind.

"I said, is this where you want to be Moselle? Either you answer me or I'm gonna make the decision for you."

"Hey man, don't talk to her like that," Majid said. He clinched and unclenched his fists.

"This really ain't 'bout you dawg; this is between me and her. But don't let my question fool you, 'cause I can make it 'bout you," Shiloh said through clinched teeth.

"Moselle, tell this man it's over between the two of you so he can leave," Majid said.

"Naw, dawg. Why don't *you* man the hell up and tell me. You want my woman; be a man and say so."

Majid's jaw tightened. He wanted so badly to take his fist to Shiloh's face, but Mo's presence made him stand down.

"What's the matter, cat go your tongue?" Shiloh taunted.

"Ain't shit got my tongue," Majid hurled back. "We can take this outside if you want."

Shiloh took a deep breath and as he did he moved so close to Majid's face the hair on the back of his neck stood up.

"I would take nothin' but pleasure in beatin' yo punk ass," Shiloh said. "You want her? Why the hell didn't you step to me like a man instead of sneakin' around behind my back with her?"

"What, she tell you *she* was gonna handle things? She tell you *she* was gonna break it off?" He continued.

"Shiloh, please!" Moselle interjected between sobs.

"No, I'm gone' tell you what happened," Shiloh continued, "you ain't man enough to handle yours. You send a woman to do your work. Well, she can have you 'cause evidently she was mistaken about me. I'm a man and you ain't nothin' but a punk-ass bitch."

Majid felt his adrenaline kick up five notches, and he cocked his head to the side and sized Shiloh up. He knew in his heart of hearts this was one fight he'd lose but his pride took over and blinded him.

Before reasoning could stop him, he hurled a punch Shiloh's way. But instead of it connecting with Shiloh's chin the way he expected, his fist was caught mid air.

Majid's knees buckled and in a split second he found himself face down in the carpet. A moan left his throat as Shiloh tightened his grip on his hand and arm.

"I will break your fuckin' arm. But because I love that woman over there, I'm gonna spare you. If I ever see your punk-ass again, I promise you, I will finish this."

Releasing Majid, Shiloh stood to his feet and turned to Moselle. "You clearly are not the woman I thought you were, and to think I was going to ask you to be my wife and help me raise my son."

He paused as he looked her up and down. "I don't ever want to see you again. Stay away from me and Tristan. Don't call or text me. As a matter of fact, lose my number."

The sound of the door as it closed behind Shiloh seemed louder to Moselle than it actually was. She looked at Majid, covered her face and released the tears she thought were all cried out.

Chapter 27

Shiloh opened the door to his home and sat down in his den. He was thankful for the quiet as Tristan was with his parents. The war that raged in his heart threatened to tear it open.

He couldn't believe he'd been so stupid. Were there signs that he refused to acknowledge, things he'd purposely overlooked when it came to Moselle? He knew she seemed distant, but there had to be more.

His mind drifted to Angela for a minute. He knew there was nothing between them. So being unfaithful, yeah... he could see her doing that. After all, they weren't an item. What he never imagined her doing was abandoning Tristan.

"How could you be a fool twice man?" He said to himself.

Shiloh stood and walked into his office. He sat at his desk and opened the center drawer. He stared at the velvet box before he pulled it out and opened it. The emerald shaped one carat diamond shimmered in the light. He knew he should pray, but the pain in his heart felt as though it cut his words off.

The first tear fell and he did nothing to stop the cascade that followed. Shiloh leaned his head back against his chair and wept. Moselle was the first woman he'd loved in a long time. And the first he'd allowed into his life completely in years.

When his first love broke his heart, he swore he'd not go down that road again. He swore he'd be more careful but here he was.

The sound of the doorbell startled Shiloh and he sat up and wiped his face with the back of his hand. He glanced at the clock on his desk and wondered who could be ringing his bell at ten o'clock at night. One thing he knew for sure, it better not be Moselle.

He stopped in the bathroom off of his office, splashed cold water on his face and quickly dried it before he answered the door.

When he glanced through the peep, he was surprised to see his mother standing there especially without Tristan.

"Mom! Is everything alright? Where's Tristan and dad?"

"Everything is just fine with the baby; I left him with your Father." Ines said as she stepped around her son. "Now, let's talk about you," she added.

After she prepared both of them a cup of tea, she led the way out onto the sun porch. Ines allowed the silence that followed to settle between them for a few minutes. She knew Shiloh had trouble expressing himself when he was hurting, but tonight she was not going to give him a chance to mill over it.

There was an urgency here that had to be attended to in order for the outcome already set in motion to be fulfilled. She took a sip of her tea and then set the cup down.

"Tell me what happened tonight," Ines said

Shiloh took a deep breath. The last thing he wanted to do was discuss the drama that just befell him. "What makes you think something happened, Mom?"

Ines turned to face Shiloh head on. "Son, every since you were born I've known when things were bothering you. I may not know exactly what happened, but I can feel it in here when you're disturbed." She laid her hand on top of her heart.

Her son closed his eyes and momentarily turned away. He knew there was no getting around this conversation; he just didn't want to have it tonight.

"I really don't feel up to discussing the situation tonight, Mom."

"Okay, well then, just listen."

"*Oh lawd . . .*" Shiloh mumbled under his breath and rolled his eyes.

"I know you don't want to hear this son because you're in pain, but while a wound is fresh is the best time to begin treating it."

Ines paused to give her son a minute to accept the fact that she would have her say. When he opened his eyes and looked at her, the tears that brimmed his lids did not deter her.

"Shiloh baby," she started as she took his hand. "Sometimes people make terrible mistakes. Mistakes so bad that once they realize it was a mistake, they wish they could undo what's done." She paused again.

"It may take us some time to come to grips with our misconception concerning the decision, but we usually do. And when we do, we need forgiveness from those we've wronged."

Shiloh sighed but he didn't speak. "Baby," Ines said, "One day you will see that in order to receive our full blessings, we must let go."

Raising Tristan

There was no doubt in Shiloh's mind that his mother had some sort of idea he and Moselle had broken up. But tonight was not the night for forgiveness in his mind – tonight or any other night for that matter. As a matter of fact, the woman he loved and planned on marrying - giving herself to another man in his book was beyond forgiveness.

Chapter 28

Four months had come and gone since Shiloh's breakup with Moselle. Although he still thought of her and he still hurt, he was grateful the pain in his heart had become more of a dull ache instead of the constant throbbing he felt in the beginning.

Tristan was now sixteen months old and two hands full. Shiloh rarely got a moment to himself once he got in from work but he didn't mind. His son was the "apple of his eye," and the one constant in his life that kept him sane.

Raising Tristan

It seemed to Shiloh, Tristan never learned to walk but instead took off running from age fourteen months old when he took his first step until now. *"Boy, when you become a teenager, I can see you gonna have to be watched closely,"* Shiloh would say to himself with a chuckle once Tristan feel asleep.

Since his breakup with Moselle, Shiloh's Friday and Saturday nights meant a good movie, wings from his favorite kitchen ('Ines' place') and a cold beer. His mother either barbequed them Cajun style or fried them. She usually made a batch of seasoned fries and a tossed salad for her son as well.

"You need to get out and meet someone baby," Ines always said on her way out the door, although she knew Shiloh wouldn't.

"Who is gonna watch my son while I date Mom? Besides, I'm content here with my boy."

"Your father and I will be more than happy to baby sit anytime and you know it."

"I'm good Ma," he replied as he gave her a good night kiss. "Besides, I'd have to share my wings and you know I don't do well with sharing."

"Ummmm hummmm," Ines sighed as she closed the door behind her and headed to her car and home.

Just as his mother shut the door, Shiloh heard Tristan yell for him. "Da-daah, da-daah!"

"I'm coming little man!" He said with a laugh and headed toward the kitchen to grab Tristan and his wings.

Chapter 29

"Mom, I think I'm going to find a nice daycare for Tristan this week. I've heard about some reputable centers, so I'm going to take a couple days off and take a look. But I want you to come with me." Shiloh said to his mother over Sunday dinner.

Robert Milner, Shiloh's father, grabbed the table and braced for impact. As he did, he gave his son a look of warning. Ines almost choked on her chicken and had to take a drink of water to stop the coughing fit that followed Shiloh's statement.

"You gonna do what?" Ines asked once she regained her ability to talk.

"I was thinking about finding a daycare center for Tristan. It's so you and Dad can have some free time, Mom, and travel when you need to."

"We aren't going anywhere our grandbaby can't come, are we Robert?" Ines said with conviction.

"No, ma'am." Robert replied. He winked at his son and smiled.

"So, why you think you need a sitter Shiloh? We don't use sitters in this family. You know that." Ines asked her son.

Shiloh sighed. "Mom, it's just as I said. You and dad need a break sometime. Plus you need to take a trip home and see about Aunt Bree. Boo-Boo said she's been asking for you and you know she's not well, Mother."

"Son, there is no reason Tristan couldn't come with us if we run home to see my sister. Besides, the family wants to see how big he's gotten anyway." Ines countered.

"Mother, I love you and I trust you with my life and Tristan's but you are not taking my son to Louisiana without me. He isn't ready for that kind of trip yet and you know it."

Ines sighed and primped her lips. "Come on mom," Shiloh started as he took his mother's hand, "you know this is a good idea. You've been supportive of me and Tristan since

Angela walked out on us. I want to do something for you and dad to thank you."

"I am thanked son. You don't need to do anything special."

"Your mother's right, Shiloh, we do what we do because we love you and you're our son." Robert added.

Shiloh smiled. "I know Dad but still, I've done well in life because you and mom poured unselfishly into me and the time has come for me to start blessing you."

With that being said, Shiloh stepped out of the kitchen and returned in a couple minutes with an envelope. He placed it in his mother's hand. "Open it."

Ines looked from Shiloh to Robert. "What have you gone and done son?" she asked.

"Open it Mom. Please Dad, you switch seats with me so you can see." Shiloh said as he stood to his feet. Once he and his father had traded places at the table, Shiloh nodded to his mother to open the envelope.

When Ines saw the contents, her hand flew to her mouth. "Can you afford this Son?" she asked.

"Mother, yes I can. You and dad taught me well. Dad, you especially taught me to provide for my family. You two and Tristan are my family."

Robert smiled at Shiloh and nodded. "I'm proud of you," he said to Shiloh. "Ines, you been complaining about being tired and wanting to go home for a while; now is your chance."

"Well, I'm proud of you too," Ines added, "But I still want to know if you can afford this?"

"Mom, I may have done some things that I'm not too proud of over the past few years, but one thing I did do was to manage my money well, just as you taught me." Shiloh shrugged his shoulders.

"I recently opened a third auto repair shop and I'm about to open a fourth one in Hampton under a local manager there," He continued, "So, it's kinda like my first franchise."

Robert was quiet but his face beamed with pride.

"Yes, baby I understand all of that but this is two plane tickets to N'awlins and a check for $1,000.00!"

Shiloh smiled. "Oh boy. Can you help me out Dad?"

"Ines, look at me," Robert touched his wife's cheek and gently turned her face to his. "Our son has done well for himself. Now, we raised him to be the type of man that he is and he is trying to bless us. Let him baby."

Looking from her husband to her son, Ines' eyes filled with tears. "Okay," she finally agreed. "But where are you going to find a daycare center for Tristan in two weeks time?"

"I have some good leads, Mom. Remember, some of my guys have children. Mack, my head mechanic at the Eastern Henrico site, had a great recommendation from his wife. I'm going to check it out tomorrow."

Now it was Ines' turn to beam with pride. "You've become more of a man than I could have asked; good for you baby." She leaned over and kissed Shiloh on the check. "Thank you son, I'm going to enjoy this visit with my sister. And maybe Brother will come down from Mississippi and join us."

Chapter 30

Shiloh approached the *A Good Morning Start Daycare* early the next morning. He made a last minute decision to make the appointment alone. He felt it would allow him to pay closer attention to the staff and routines at the facility without Tristan.

The other thing he wanted to prevent was Tristan's presence becoming a distraction. He didn't want the staff doting over his son in such as way as to deter him from observing their interactions with the children in their care.

"Good morning! May I help you?" A perky young lady who appeared to be around twenty years old asked from behind a desk as soon as Shiloh entered the building.

"Yes, my name is Shiloh Milner and I have an appointment with the director."

"Okay, Mr. Milner. May I ask the nature of your visit?"

Shiloh smiled; he liked the fact that the receptionist questioned his intentions. "I'm here to interview for a space in your Center for my son."

"That's great. May I see your driver's license or a picture I.D. please?"

He handed her his driver's license as requested. The young lady glanced from the photograph on the license to Shiloh to ensure he was who he said he was. Once she was satisfied, she extended her hand in a greeting.

"My name is Mandy. I will need to hold onto your I.D. until after your visit. Please sign in and grab a visitor's badge. Our director is out for the day, but our assistant director, Ms. Brown, will see you. Just a moment please, while I announce you."

In a matter of seconds, Shiloh was buzzed into the interior of the center where he was met by a young man by the name of Matt who escorted him to Ms. Brown's office.

Shiloh spent the next forty-five minutes speaking with the assistant director about their facility and what they had to offer his son.

He was given a tour and allowed to spend about fifteen minutes in the classroom with the children Tristan's age. Matt suddenly appeared and sat with teacher's assistant while Ms. Cumberland, who would be Tristan's lead teacher, joined Shiloh and Ms. Brown back in the office. This allowed Shiloh to ask questions of the teacher as well.

When he was satisfied and had asked all of his questions for the moment, he was escorted back to the entrance where he signed out and his license was returned.

"So, is this your routine for all visitors?" He asked Mandy.

"Yes it is. Our policy firmly enforces safety for our children. I've been with *A Good Morning Start* for two years now and we've never had a problem.

Until the staff is familiar with our parents, we ask for I.D. and escort them to their child's room. Our philosophy behind that is a staff member may be off or on vacation when a child starts and not be familiar with a parent. So, we don't just take their word for who they say they are. We make sure.

Our pick-up routine is just as careful. Parents are required to show I.D. and sign in. Their names are checked against a file containing a copy of their license before they are buzzed back." Mandy said matter of fact.

"Wow, I like that. My son won't be full time but I like knowing that when he is here, I don't have to worry." Shiloh said with a smile.

"Great! I hope you choose us. You won't be disappointed."

"I think I already have," Shiloh replied on his way out the door.

After Shiloh enrolled Tristan in *A Good Morning Start*, at the prompting of Ines, he decided to do a trial run with Tristan spending a few hours at the Center. Although he knew his son would be fine, he agreed. Shiloh realized it was more for his mother's benefit than his son's.

Tristan seemed a little reluctant to stay when he first got to his room. But after seeing all the toys and new faces to play with, he settled in. Ines, on the other hand, cried all the way back home.

"I can't believe my baby's in daycare," she said tearfully.

"Mom, think of it this way, Tristan has other children to play with which we both know is good for him. And, now he has somewhere safe to stay if you and Dad ever need a break or have some place to go you can't take him."

"There is no place I go that my baby can't go." Ines snapped. "You young people and leaving your children with stranger's git on my nerves."

Shiloh smiled. "Mom, now you know I don't leave my son with strangers. You and Dad have been his caretakers since birth."

"Mom . . ." Shiloh said quietly, "You need this vacation and Aunt Bree is sick. She's been asking for you; she needs her big sister."

"I know," Ines managed to say between tears, "It just seems once you started school, next thing I knew you were a man. I just don't want my grandbaby growing up on me as fast as you did."

"Come on mom, Tristan is just a baby. He's not even two yet."

"Eighteen months, or two years, what's the difference?"

"Okay, Mom. You're over reacting. Tristan won't be in daycare everyday, just every now and again when we need it. And as you always taught me, it's better to have and not need than to need and not have."

Ines finally smiled, but more so at her son using her words to make a point rather than feeling better. Several hours later when they picked Tristan up from *A Good Morning Start*, he was no worse for the wear from the brief visit and neither was Ines.

Chapter 31

The time for Ines' and Robert's visit seem to come out of nowhere. Shiloh and Tristan took them to the airport and sat with them until it was time to board.

Ines made Shiloh promise to call her nightly with a report on her grandson's day and so she could say goodnight to him. Of course, Shiloh agreed with a smile.

Early the next morning, Shiloh and Tristan headed to *A Good Morning Start*. Shiloh was a bit more nervous this time. Perhaps, it was knowing his parents were miles away and he was now on his own with Tristan. Perhaps it was leaving his son in the care of someone other than his mother for the first time. Whatever it was, it caused Shiloh to be a bit anxious.

"Good morning Mr. Milner!" Mandy greeted him with a warm and welcoming smile. "And good morning to you too, Mr. Tristan."

Shiloh signed himself and Tristan in and proceeded to Tristan's classroom. After his son was settled, he was approached my Matt. "Excuse me Mr. Milner but our director Ms. Paynne would like to see you."

As he followed Matt down the narrow hallway, Shiloh wondered what the meeting was about. "Ah Matt, can you tell me what this is about? I need to head on into work."

Shiloh thought about the new mechanic he had starting today. The guy was good but fresh out of school. His usual trainer was out on sick leave, and Shiloh didn't trust anyone else to oversee.

"She just wants to say hello and welcome you; it won't take long," Matt said with a smile as he opened the door to the director's office.

When Ms. Paynne turned around, Shiloh had to work to hide his surprise. "Shelly?" he asked as he approached her desk.

"Shiloh! It is you, what a wonderful surprise. When I saw your son's last name, I thought maybe, but what were the odds."

Shelly Paynne's smile was as brilliant as Shiloh remembered and as he glanced at her left hand so were the diamonds on her ring finger. Her pretty cinnamon complexioned face hadn't aged a day although it had been eighteen years since they'd seen each other.

At one point in time, Shelly was the love of Tristan's life. And he swore his heart skipped a beat when she wrapped her arms around him and embraced him in a warm hug.

"You look great Shell," he said as his eyes took in her curves. Her waist was still tiny as ever and her hips and round derrière seemed to have the firmness of a twenty-five year old woman, instead of one of forty-five. Her breasts appeared to perk up in his presence.

"And you don't look too shabby yourself, Shi," she said as she pulled him into her dimples he used to take pleasure in kissing.

"So," Shelly started breaking the spell between them that made it clear the attraction was still there after the years. "Your little one is here on an as-necessary basis, huh?"

"Yeah," Shiloh took a seat and then continued, "My mother usually keeps him while I work but she and my dad are on vacation. I needed a safe place to take him when they're busy or need a break."

"Well, I'm happy you chose us . . . Is he your only one or you probably have some school age children running around by now, huh?" Shelly said as she glanced at his ring finger.

"No, he's my one and only. I guess I started late." Shiloh smiled. "How about you, you got any kids?"

Shelly turned away. "No, we don't have any but I do have two stepsons," she replied quietly. It was obvious she was uncomfortable with the question.

"I didn't mean to upset you with my question; I thought we were catching up."

"No, I'm good," She said as she turned to face Shiloh, "Besides all the babies here are mine."

Just as Shiloh opened his mouth to speak, his cell phone rang; it was his Chesterfield shop. "I apologize but I have to take this."

"Well, I've got to run, Shelly," he said after he disconnected the call. "I have a new employee starting today and he's waiting on me."

"New employee?" Shelly said with a look that expressed curiosity as well as pride.

"Yes, I own four auto repair shops: one in Chesterfield and one each in Eastern and Western Henrico counties and a new one in Hampton. *R&S Auto*, perhaps, you've heard of me?" He said as he handed her his card.

Shelly looked at the business card with pride, "*R&S Auto. Shiloh Milner, Co-Owner.* Wow, I'm impressed. Actually, I have heard of you. Your shops specialize in the repair of foreign vehicles right?"

"Yes, we do. My dad is my partner but he's retired now. He sits home and collects a check." Shiloh said with a laugh.

"How are your parents?" Shelly asked as she walked him to the door.

"They're great Shell. I'll tell them you're here. My mother will rest much easier knowing that. She about had a meltdown when I told her I was thinking about putting Tristan in daycare."

"Okay one more question for you." Shelly started before she opened her office door, "Is there no Mrs. Milner?"

Shiloh swore he saw a twinkle in her eyes as she spoke. "No Shelly, there is no Mrs. Milner. I'm a single dad. But that's a story for another time," he added. He knew she was curious.

"I'm just asking."

He looked at her and chuckled as he turned to exit her office and the building. "What?" she asked.

"You haven't changed one bit in that department," he responded. With that, he offered her one last smile, turned and headed to work.

"See you later Mr. Milner!" Mandy said as enthusiastically as she had when Shiloh dropped Tristan off.

"Yup, see ya later Mandy. Take extra good care of my son."

"We will!"

Chapter 32

Shiloh phoned his parents after he had dinner and settled Tristan down for the night. "Hi Mom! How was your flight?"

"It was good baby. First class was nice and we had a great flight attendant. Now, how was my grandbaby's first day?"

"It went well. He did fine when I dropped him off; I on the other hand, was a tad bit nervous."

"Not you?" His mother ribbed.

"Yes Mother, me." Shiloh chuckled.

"Well, was Tristan okay when you picked him up?"

"He sure was. His teacher said he did very well." Shiloh said and Ines smiled.

"Oh yes," Shiloh started. He paused to take a sip of his water. "Do you remember Shelly Paynne?"

"How could I not? She was the love of your life at one point."

"Well, she's the head of *A Good Morning Start*. Isn't that great? I was so surprised to see her. But now that I know she's there, I feel better about leaving Tristan."

Ines paused, "Be careful, Shiloh."

"What do you mean by that Mom?

"I'm just saying, be careful Son."

"Mom, I know you. Those words have a lot more meaning than just 'be careful.' So, what are you getting at?"

"You and Shelly have history and I sense the attraction is still there."

Shiloh was quiet for a few minutes. "I appreciate your concern Mom, but Shelly is happily married and I'm taking a break from relationships. I just thought if you knew she was there, since you already know her, you'd feel better about Tristan attending daycare."

"I do feel better baby. I just remember you and Shelly had quite an intense romance and sometimes those types of relationships don't die easily."

"I hear you Mom. I'll keep that thought in the back of my mind. Now, how is Aunt Bree?" He asked hoping to change the subject.

"Bree is coming along. Things aren't as bad as I thought but she's still not well. I'm glad you insisted I come."

Shiloh smiled, "Me too Mom. Now, where is Dad?"

"Oh, your father is out with his oldest brother and a couple of his cousins. They went for drinks and to play some pool."

"Good for Dad. Well Mom, I'm going to get off the phone; I have a movie I want to check out. Enjoy your stay and use the money I gave you to do some fun things for you and dad."

"Shiloh, I know you changed the subject because you don't want to hear what I have to say about you and Shelly. But I hope you do keep it in mind."

"Mom, all my life you've been here for me, and you usually have your say about things. Right now I'm trying to get over Moselle, who by the way, you said was for me. And look how *that* turned out. I appreciate your *'gift'* Ma, but this time, I think I'm good."

Ines was speechless for a minute. *"Did my Son just tell me off in a nice way?"* She said to herself.

"Ma, you there?"

"Yes, I'm here Shiloh."

He could hear the change in his mother's tone. "I apologize if I offended you Mom, that wasn't my intention. I just don't feel up to hearing a lecture tonight."

"I understand. No offense taken. You and Tristan have a good night. By the way where is my grandson? I'm supposed to say goodnight to him."

"Just a minute, I'll put the phone to his ear."

After Ines had said her goodnights to a sleeping Tristan and her son, she and Shiloh disconnected the call. She knew her son was in pain. She just didn't want him hurt anymore. But never the less, she had heard his message loud and clear and from that moment on decided to stay out of Shiloh's affairs.

Chapter 33

"Shiloh, do you have a minute?" Shelly called to him as he dropped Tristan off one morning.

"I do. Is something wrong with Tristan?" he asked concerned. "Has he done something?"

"No, it has nothing to do with that. Wait for me in my office; I'll only be a minute or two."

Five minutes later she appeared. "Sorry to keep you waiting. Now, you and Tristan have been coming here for two weeks, how do you like it?"

Shiloh tilted his head to the side and frowned at Shelly. For some reason, her question seemed bogus as if she really wanted to ask his something else.

"Well, I think we both like it here. Tristan is calm and happy when I pick him up in the afternoons, and he seems well cared for. I have no complaints."

"Good." Shelly said with a smile. The silence that followed was awkward.

"So, is that it or did you need something else?" Shiloh finally asked.

"Yes. Are you free for lunch today?" Shelly blurted out with a look of embarrassment.

Shiloh smiled. "Are you asking me out, Ms. Paynne?"

"Well, no . . . I just wondered if you wanted to grab lunch; I mean if you're free."

His smile deepened, "Sure, I'm free. Where would you like to meet, or I can pick you up."

"Ah no, we can meet. How about *Mama J's* downtown?"

"Shelly, why are we going all the way downtown for lunch when we're in Chesterfield County? They have plenty of places here." Shiloh asked with a puzzled expression.

"I thought you were working your Eastern Henrico shop today and it wouldn't be that far for you."

This time Shiloh took a seat on the edge of Shelly's desk. "Okay, tell me what this is really about Shell, 'cause my BS meter is buzzing."

Shelly closed the door to her office and sat in the chair facing Shiloh. "I don't like my employees in my business. The last thing I need is for one of them to come into a restaurant over this side of town and see us eating together," she said.

"Well, I guess that's understandable. I can meet you for lunch but downtown is a bit far for me. Although you're right about the location I'm working today. How about a nice spot in Eastern Henrico? There are some nice eateries in that area."

"Okay, that will work. When is it good for you?" Shelly asked with a grin.

Shiloh paused. It was as if he noticed Shelly for the first time that day. The way her lip gloss shined as she spoke seemed to draw him in, and he found himself wanting to kiss her.

The touch of her hand on his leg startled him back to reality. "I'm sorry, did you say something?" he asked.

"Yes, I asked you what time is good for you for lunch."

"I'm my own boss baby girl; whatever is good for you is good for me."

The smile that crossed Shelly's lips made her mouth more inviting. And for a minute, Shiloh forgot she was married.

Raising Tristan

The two met for lunch at a little greasy spoon on Williamsburg Road in Eastern Henrico close to the city line. It was a place Shiloh's employees had often raved about but he'd never tried. It proved to be the perfect setting for Shelly and Shiloh as they laughed and joked freely over their meal.

When lunch was over, Shelly asked Shiloh if he would join her again sometime. His answer was yes, and with a smile. Later that night as Shiloh sat in his home office reviewing documentation for his Hampton business, his cell phone rang. He grabbed it before he looked at the caller ID.

"Hello?"

"Hi, Shiloh?"

He glanced at the caller ID this time as the voice was unfamiliar. "Yes, this is Shiloh and to whom am I speaking?" he asked.

"This is Shelly Paynne. Am I disturbing you?"

"Shelly?" he repeated, "Uh, no you aren't disturbing me but . . ." Shiloh glanced at his watch; it was ten o'clock.

"I guess you're wondering why I'm calling you at home, huh?"

"Yeah, kinda," he said with a bit of concern in his voice.

Shelly was quiet for a minute but it seemed much longer to Shiloh. "Are you there?" he asked.

"Yes, I'm here . . . Shiloh, I called because, I need someone to talk to and well I thought of you."

Now it was Shiloh's turn to be silent. "Shiloh?"

"Yeah, I'm here. But, I'm confused."

"I know, I know; this is kinda weird. It's just that I remember how patient you were with me when I was troubled. I just need someone to talk to if it's not too much trouble."

Shiloh knew the million dollar question should have been, *"Where is your husband and why aren't you talking with him?"* But he chose to ignore his gut and lend an ear.

It was close to midnight when Shiloh and Shelly finally ended their conversation. Although he knew it was dead wrong, Shiloh fell into bed that night with a rise in his pajamas and a smile on his face; he and Shelly still clicked. His mother's voice entered his mind but he quickly shut it out. The one thing he did acknowledge, however, before he closed his eyes was the need to attend church more often.

A business relationship with Shelly Paynne was one thing but deep in the back of his mind, Shiloh knew he wanted more.

Chapter 34

Tristan clapped his little hands and squealed with delight when he saw his grandparents approaching. Ines' and Robert's vacation was a good one, but they were happy and excited to be home.

Robert's face beamed with pride when Tristan practically leaped into his arms. He turned to his wife and made a cute face as he hugged his grandson tight. As if on cue and not to leave her out, Tristan scrambled from Robert's arms into Ines' and lay his head on her shoulder.

"Look's like somebody missed you too," Shiloh said as he, too, embraced his parents. "Let's head over to the baggage claim area and get your bags, and then I'm taking you two out for dinner," he finished.

The chatter between the family was endless over dinner with Tristan even chiming in with his toddler words. Shiloh couldn't remember being more excited to have his parents with him. The support they offered him as a single father was priceless.

"Shiloh, why don't you and Tristan spend the night tonight?" Ines asked. "We can sit up late and catch up."

"No Mom, I have to be in the shop extra early tomorrow. I have a new receptionist starting and I want to make sure she's straight."

"What has that got to do with where you sleep? You can get up early here. Just go home and get your uniform and by the time you get back, I'll have Tristan down and your bed all turned back." Ines offered.

It was obvious to Shiloh his mother missed him and just wanted a little more time. "Okay, Mom," he said with a smile. "I'll grab Tristan's stuff too while I'm at it. Now, do you want me to stop by the store and pick up some breakfast food? After all you've been gone for a month; I'm sure there's nothing here."

"Oh yes baby that would be lovely. Do you need anything special Robert?" she asked her husband.

"No, I can't think of anything," Robert replied between tickling Tristan.

"Well then, I'll be back as soon as I can," Shiloh said. He bent down and kissed his son on the forehead. Tristan barely noticed Shiloh as the toddler was engrossed in play with his grandfather.

As Shiloh backed his car out the driveway, his cell phone rang. He hit the phone icon on his steering wheel and placed the call on speaker phone. "Hey, what's up Boo?!"

"Sup dawg! My auntie and uncle make it back safely?'

"Yup, they sure did. I'm just leaving them on my way home to grab a change of clothes."

"I sure am glad they came down, man. Mama really enjoyed having her sister around. I do believe it's what helped her improve."

"No doubt, dawg, no doubt."

"So, when you an' lil' man gonna make that trip?" Boo-Boo asked.

"I'm thinkin' the next few months. Tristan will be two soon, so sometime after that."

"Sweet. Well, I got this lil' cutie waitin' on a brotha, so I'll holla at chu later."

"Alright, don't get yourself hemmed up again dawg. You already got two kids; you don't need three."

"Naw, man . . . I use two rubbers dawg. This cutie swears she's on that shot, but I don't trust her any further that I can throw her and you know I likes my women with some meat on they bones."

"Ummm hummm, so I know you can't pick her up."

The cousins chuckled before they said their goodbyes and hung up the phone. As soon as Boo-Boo was gone, Shiloh's phone rang again. He thought it was his cousin calling back because he forgot something.

"Yo, what you forget dawg?" Shiloh asked.

"Excuse me?" A female voice said.

"Shelly?"

"Yes, who did you think it was?" she asked.

"Well, I was just talking with my cousin from N'awlins and I thought he was calling me back."

"Oh, is everything okay?"

"Yeah, he was just callin' to see if my parents made it home okay."

Shelly paused. "So, does this mean Tristan will be leaving us?" She asked. The change in her tone was obvious and Shiloh picked up on it right away.

"Yes, Shelly. He's only on an as needed basis, remember?"

"Well, when is his last day?" She sounded as if she were going to cry.

"It's tomorrow, Shell. But he will be there as my parents or I need him to be . . . Okay, where you goin' with all this?" He asked.

"I guess . . ."

"You guess what?" Shiloh probed.

"I thought I'd get to see you a little longer."

Shiloh frowned. "Shelly, what do you mean by that, see me a little longer?"

"Seeing you cheers me up Shiloh, I actually enjoy your conversation, ya know?"

He knew he was opening a Pandora's Box but Shiloh decided to push a little harder. "I know we're friends Shelly but this sounds like a little more to me. Am I wrong?"

She was silent for a minute as if she need time to choose her words carefully. "I need to share some things with you but not on the phone. Can you do lunch tomorrow?"

"What time?"

"How about one?"

"That'll work. Now, I gotta run. I'm picking up a few things from the store for my parents before heading back."

"Okay, see you tomorrow?" She asked as if she needed confirmation he hadn't changed his mind that quickly.

"You got it."

At exactly twelve forty-five the next afternoon, Shiloh's employee by the name of Clarence came to get him. Clarence was an older gentleman who often shared a word or two of wisdom with Shiloh.

"Shiloh . . . Shiloh!" Clarence called out as he leaned down next to the car Shiloh was working under.

"Yeah Clarence, what is it?"

"There's a woman here to see you."

Shiloh appeared with a puzzled look on his face. He knew he had a date with Shelly, but they had agreed to meet at the greasy spoon near by. *"Perhaps it's someone with a question"* he thought to himself.

"Clarence, did you ask her what she needed? Is it something you can help her with?" Shiloh sounded a bit annoyed.

"Now, you know danged well if I coulda' helped her I would. She specifically asked for you." Clarence replied equally annoyed at being questioned.

"Okay, tell her I'll be right there," Shiloh said as he wiped his hands. He silently hoped this wouldn't take long. He was cutting it close as it was for his rendezvous with Shelly.

When he approached the entrance to the shop, he recognized the body of the woman straight away. "Shelly? What are you doing here? Is everything okay?"

She knew he meant with his son. "Tristan is fine. I was able to get away a little early and so I decided to see if you wanted to ride with me?" She replied.

Shiloh couldn't figure out what it was at that moment that was any different from the other times he laid eyes on Shelly. But for some reason, today she looked especially sexy.

When he glanced over his shoulder, he noticed every man in the bay had stopped what he was doing and stared at her. He grabbed her by the elbow and quickly pulled her around the side of the building to where her car was parked.

"Why don't I meet you there as planned? Besides, I need to clean up a bit. You go on and get us a table," he said as he opened the door to her car.

On his way to his office, Shiloh bumped into Clarence, literally. "Whoa, sorry C, I wasn't paying attention to where I was going."

"That woman is ah Si-reen, Shiloh. You best leave her be."

Shiloh frowned. "Ah Siren?" He said and then chuckled. "You sound like some of those old country folk from N'awlins, C. Ah Siren."

"You can laugh if you want, Shiloh, but you know I'm right. And you know you wrong." Clarence said and then spit a glop of brown saliva in a can he carried.

"Damm C! Will you stop chewin' that nasty stuff! Shiloh chastised.

"Ain't nothin' wrong with my chewin' ta-bacco," Clarence said, "sides, this ain't 'bout me and my habit, this 'bout you an that Si-reen," he finished as he pointed to Shiloh's chest.

"I appreciate your concern Pop," A nick-name Shiloh gave Clarence that was now used around the shop, "But we're just friends."

"Well," Clarence started and then spit, "She may be a friend in your book, but she lookin' for a little more than that from you." He finished followed by more spitting.

"I don't think so, Pop but I'll keep that in mind. Now, if you'll excuse me, I need to wash up a bit and grab some lunch."

Clarence took his time and spit one more glob of tobacco juice into his can before he turned to leave. As he did, he made eye contact with Shiloh and muttered, "Ummm hummm."

Chapter 36

"Sorry I'm late," Shiloh apologized as he slid into the seat opposite Shelly. "I got held up after you left. Have you ordered yet?"

"No, I don't have much appetite," she replied, "I'm just having a small salad and water."

Just as she finished her sentence, the server came and took their order.

"So, what is it you have to tell me?" Shiloh asked. "I don't have as much time as I usually do. I have to finish up a car and then head over to the West-End."

Shelly took a deep breath. "I miss you, Shiloh." She looked away for a minute and then continued. "I never should have agreed to our break-up."

Shiloh took her hands into his. "That was a long time ago, Shell, and it was for the best. You were moving to Italy, remember?"

"Yes, I remember . . . But still, I wish we had tried."

"Shelly, a long distance relationship is one thing, but Europe is something entirely different."

"You could have come with me," she said. Her voice started to quiver and she fought to keep it steady.

Shiloh shook his head. "You know that was impossible; it wasn't in the plans for me at the time. You needed to do you."

The server showed up with their meals just as Shiloh was about to speak. They allowed the young man to arrange their food and ask if they needed anything else. Both replied, no.

"Look at you, Shell. You've done well for yourself. Two years abroad, a Master's degree, a husband, you should be proud."

"He doesn't love me like you did."

Her comment caught Shiloh off guard and it took him a second or two to regroup. "Shelly, those are strong words. You don't mean that."

"Yes, I do. Nicholas is a good provider and I have everything I need but he doesn't love me . . . not like you did. Not from here," she said as she placed her hand over her heart.

"Have you talked to him about your feelings?"

"Of course I have. And before you say it, we've been to counseling too. Nothing changes."

"Wow . . . I'm sorry to hear that."

"That's why I've been calling you; I just need to hear your voice sometimes. Besides, Nik's never home anyway; he travels all the time for his business."

Shiloh was quiet. He wanted to allow her to finish and he needed time to choose his words carefully. "Shell, I'm flattered but—"

"I'm not asking you for anything Shiloh. I just need a friend, that's all. Just a friend," she finished quietly.

"Well, I guess there's nothing wrong with that."

"So, I can call you every now and again?" her tone brightened.

"Sure, every now and again."

Raising Tristan

"Thanks," Shelly said and glanced at her watch. "I guess you better get back, we've been gone about forty-five minutes. Besides, I'll see you in a few hours when you pick up Tristan."

"I'm not picking up Tristan today; my parents are. I've got to go to Hampton tonight for an early morning meeting tomorrow."

It took a second before Shelly was able to gather herself. The disappointment on her face was obvious. "Oh, I see . . . Well, may I call you tonight? Besides, I want to know why a man as fine and as put together as you is single."

Shiloh chuckled. "I'm single by choice. I've chosen to concentrate on raising my son. I don't want a lot of women in and out of his life."

"Who said it had to be a lot of women. It could be one special lady," Shelly teased with a wink of her eye.

The smile on Shiloh's lips let her know he knew she was trying to get all up in his business and although his instincts warned him, he decided at that moment to let her.

Chapter 37

Shiloh chose to leave late that night for Hampton after Tristan was down for the night. It was not the first time he'd left his son with his parents, but it was the first time he'd traveled out of town. Shiloh wanted to tuck Tristan in himself, with a promise to be home as soon as he could.

By the time he reached his hotel room and settled in it was close to eleven o'clock. He was too wired from separation anxiety to sleep, so after phoning his mother for the third time, he decided to watch some television. Just as he got into the movie he selected, his phone rang. The sound startled him and he was relieved to see it wasn't his parents.

"Hello?"

"Hey handsome, what 'cha up to?" It was Shelly and she sounded more seductive than ever.

"Just watching a movie," he replied. His hand traveled down his torso in an effort to still the rise that began in his pajamas at the sound of her voice.

"Down boy, she's married." he said to himself.

"I was just checking on you to make sure you made it okay," she said.

"Thanks, I'm good. I've only been here for about an hour. I didn't leave until Tristan was down for the night."

Shelly smiled. "You are such a good dad. The world needs more like you. I've never seen a more dedicated father; single or otherwise."

"Wow, thanks. But I'm sure you're biased." He blushed as he spoke.

"No, I see a lot of fathers and believe it or not you aren't our only single dad. But you are by far the most devoted."

"Thanks again."

Savannah J

"So, tell me about Tristan's mom; is she in the picture at all? You never mention her," Shelly said. She took a sip from her glass of wine and settled in for a bit of juicy gossip.

Shiloh took a deep breath. It had been awhile since he discussed Angela and frankly he preferred to leave it that way.

"Her name is Angela and no, she's not in the picture." He paused and Shelly waited. "Tristan's mother deserted him - well us at his birth. I haven't heard from her since."

"I am so sorry, Shi," Shelly said as she sat forward, "I didn't mean to open a wound."

"It's okay. It is what it is. Sooner or later I have to talk about how I feel; I can't keep it bottled up forever."

After hearing the beginning of the story, Shelly was remorseful she'd asked. "Listen, you really don't have to explain to me Shi. Forgive me for asking."

"No, it's time I talked about it and, perhaps, once I do it won't seem so bad."

Shiloh spent the next hour sharing his feelings with Shelly. It felt like a cleansing and she was more than eager to play his healer. When they finally hung up the phone both felt a little closer to the other.

Thirty minutes later Shiloh took a chance and called her back. When she answered he didn't say hello. He asked her a simple question, "Tell me why you never had children."

"When I got to Italy, I found out I was pregnant. Before I could tell you, I had a miscarriage. When I married Nik, I knew better than to bring children into our dysfunctional world, so I remained childless."

"Why didn't you tell me about the baby?"

"What difference would it have made, Shiloh? I lost it and you made it clear you wouldn't come to Italy! I just sucked it up and went on."

"I still would have liked to have known. Maybe . . ."

"Maybe what? We could have tried again?"

"I don't know . . . Yes, maybe yes." Both were silent for a minute. "When I look into Tristan's face there are times I see you. I see what could have been ours. I guess instinctively I knew he wasn't my first."

Shelly smiled, "You are your mother's son," she said.

"Oh lawd, don't start that." He laughed with her. "Look," he started, "I just needed to hear the truth. That day in your office when I asked you about children, I saw it in your eyes."

"Why didn't you ask me then?"

"It wasn't time."

"I still love you Shiloh Milner; you know that right?"

Shiloh paused. Moselle flashed before his face and he quickly pushed her away. "Yeah, actually, I do know."

She didn't want to hear him say he no longer loved her, so she quickly said good night and hung up the phone.

Shiloh lay back on the bed and closed his eyes. He prayed sleep would come swiftly because he needed to be saved from his thoughts and from himself.

Chapter 38

Over the next couple months the conversations between Shiloh and Shelly increased as did their lunch dates. Shiloh found himself thinking of her more often, but he also found himself missing Moselle. There were days when he wondered if Shelly had become a safe substitute for Mo, just as he had for Shelly's husband.

"May I come over?" Shelly asked one night as they were talking.

"Shelly, do you think that's wise? Besides, I have my son here with me."

Savannah J

"It's nine o'clock at night, Shiloh, he's asleep right?"

"Yes, he's asleep. But Shell, don't you think that's pushing things a bit. I mean we're friends and we talk on the phone. I don't think you coming to my home is a good idea."

"Okay, may I can drive down to Hampton this week and spend time?"

"Okay, where are you going with this?"

"Shiloh, it's no secret anymore that I'm not happy and being with you makes me happy. I just want a little of your time."

"Shelly . . ."

"Just dinner, I just want to meet you for dinner. I can drive down, grab a bite and head back."

"And who is going to cover for you while you slip out of town?"

"I don't have to leave early. I can leave work around five and be in Hampton by six-thirty."

Shiloh knew immediately what she was after and although he knew it was a bad judgment call on his part, he suddenly had a burning desire to kiss Shelly.

"Okay, but just dinner and then you hit the road. If it's too late for you to drive, I'll get you a room but you are out of there in time enough to go to work."

"Deal," Shelly replied with a smile wide enough to crack her cheeks. Although she said she would work until five o'clock the day she was set to meet Shiloh, Shelly left work around three that afternoon. She headed home, showered and packed an over night bag. After she placed her things in the car, she left a note for her husband telling him she was taking a last minute out of town business trip.

As a slow desire for making love crept over her, she planned the evening and a rendezvous with Shiloh that was sure to keep her satisfied for months.

Shelly sent Shiloh a text message once she hit the Hampton City limits. He answered that he was running a bit behind but had almost finished with his meeting. He gave her the name of his hotel and instructed her to wait for him in the lobby. He promised he wouldn't be long.

The hotel where Shiloh was staying for the night had a nice restaurant and lounge, so Shelly decided to have a drink while she waited. No sooner had she finished her drink, Shiloh walked in.

Shelly turned toward a male voice when she heard her name and smiled when she noticed it was Shiloh, and the sight of him took her breath away. It had been years since Shelly had seen him in a suit, and she swore he was the most beautiful thing she'd seen in awhile.

"Hey beautiful," he said as he leaned down as kissed her cheek.

"Hey, yourself," she replied.

"I was going to ask if you wanted to freshen up before dinner," Shiloh said "but you look pretty put together."

"Thanks, I had a chance to freshen up before I left."

"Good, so are you ready for dinner?" he asked with a grin.

"Yes, but what about just staying here. We can order room service and chill in your room. I'm sure you must be tired."

Shiloh took a minute before he answered. He knew exactly where she was going with this. He realized a way out was being made for him, but lust took over and he shut the door of escape and walked head-long into the one Shelly held open for him.

Chapter 39

The minute the hotel door closed behind Shiloh and Shelly he forgot about his promise of celibacy to God and himself. He grabbed Shelly and pushed her against the door - hard. The way she held onto him showed she was more than willing to go along with the plan.

She ripped at his suit almost tearing the buttons from the expensive jacket as she tried desperately to pull it off. Shiloh paused as he stepped back and obliged her by coming out of his jacket and tie.

Shelly could feel herself grow weak with anticipation as the only man she's ever really loved prepared to satisfy her as only he could. When she started to unbutton her blouse in an effort to help things along, he grabbed her hands and stopped her.

"Let me, baby. You know I always enjoyed undressing you, that hasn't changed."

A soft groan was the only reply Shelly could manage as she realized her wait was finally over. She hadn't had a pleasing sex life with her husband in years and her body now ached with desire.

Shiloh took his time and undressed her piece by piece. When she was completely nude, he picked her up and laid her across his bed. "You are so beautiful," he whispered in her ear as he planted soft kisses along her jaw.

"Please . . ." she moaned unable to stand the wait any longer.

As he stood to his feet and began to remove his clothes, Clarence's voice came to him. *That woman is 'ah Si-reen, Shiloh. You best leave her be.*

Shiloh stopped and looked over his shoulder. He knew they were alone in the room but Clarence's voice sounded so clear for a moment, it shook him.

"Did you hear that?" he asked Shelly.

"Hear what baby?" Shelly replied. "I don't hear anything except my heartbeat, 'cause you got me so ready."

"She may be a friend in your book, but she lookin' for a little more than that from you," Clarence's voice once again spoke to Shiloh.

Shelly noticed the hesitancy in Shiloh's movements. It had been eight years since she'd been satisfied by anyone or anything other than her own hands, and she was not going to allow Shiloh to become distracted, not even by his thoughts.

"Look at me baby," she purred as she used her hands to travel the length of her body. She stopped just as they reached her feminine mound. Slowly she parted her legs, and gave him a clear view of what awaited him.

At lightening speed, the incident with Moselle and Majid passed before Shiloh's eyes and he knew he was in the room with Shelly for all the wrong reasons.

"If I do this, I'm no better than Majid," he said to himself, *"Shelly is somebody's wife."*

As much as he hated to admit it to himself, this entire thing with Shelly up to this point had been about revenge and control. It was as if he was trying to punish Moselle by being with Shelly. After all, Shelly was not only intelligent but she was beautiful, successful and wealthy.

"Forgiveness is not for the offender Shiloh, it's for us," he heard his mother's voice say. Something she'd told him many times in the past.

Shiloh sat down on the bed beside Shelly. He looked into her eyes and then pulled her to him. The way he looked at her spoke volumes and she began to weep.

"I'm so sorry baby, but I can't do this. As unhappy as you are, you're still a married woman."

He placed his hand under her chin and raised her face to his. He kissed her softly and then said, "Do you understand?"

The pain in her eyes told him that although she understood his words, her heart was broken. He pulled her to him again and held her until her tears stopped.

"Listen, I'm going to go downstairs and get myself another room. I don't want you on the road this late and this upset alone, okay?' She nodded her head.

Shiloh continued. "Take your time and get yourself together and I'll take you to dinner. Then we'll come back here and maybe watch a movie in your room until you feel like you can sleep."

As he stood to dress, Shelly said, "I don't know who she is, but she's a lucky woman."

He turned to her, "What do you mean?"

Raising Tristan

"I've held onto the dream of us for all those years, Shi. You were so good to me and I knew you loved me . . . I guess I just hoped when I ran into you again, the magic would still be there."

She paused, "When I saw you for the first time, it opened up the floodgates and all I wanted to do was fall into your arms and have you tell me everything was going to be alright."

Shiloh sat back down. "Well, I'll admit when I saw you, I had thoughts too."

"But dear heart, I also saw her in your eyes." Shelly said softly. "I guess I just hoped what we had would be enough to make you forget."

"How can you say that Shell, you're married?" Shiloh asked with a frown.

For the first time, Shelly laughed. "Do you honestly believe Nik gives a rat's . . ." she paused. "Nicholas doesn't care what I do Shiloh. God knows he's had his share of mistresses.

The one he has now, he's had for two years."

Shiloh tilted his head and regarded Shelly. "Are you telling me, you know your husband runs around on you and you're still with him?" The shock and disbelief was clearly written across his face.

She shrugged her shoulders and looked away.

"Come on babe," Shiloh said and turned her face back to his. "You have got to be kidding me, Shell. You're better than that . . . Don't you believe you are?"

"I don't know what I believe anymore. My husband doesn't put his hands on me; I have all I need; and come and go as I please."

"Shelly, that can't be enough or you wouldn't be here with me."

As if she'd noticed she was nude for the first time, Shelly pulled the bed sheet around her. "What do you want me to do Shiloh? What do you expect me to do?!" She said with tear filled eyes.

"I expect you to have more love for yourself that's what! Where did she go, huh? The young lady I fell in love with, the one who had enough guts to tour Europe for an entire year alone!"

Shelly bowed her head for a minute and said, "I guess she got lost somewhere along the way."

"Well then, I suggest you go and find her because you know what? Even if I did say yes to this affair you want with me, no one can make you happy but you. It starts here, Shelly," he said and placed his hand on her heart.

As she lifted her head and looked into his eyes, Shiloh thought he saw a hint of that young girl from long ago. "I don't know," she said.

"What happened, Shelly? How did you get here?"

"I think the question is: how did *we* get here?"

"We?" he questioned, "Don't turn this thing around Shell; we're talking about you."

"I know we are, but you are just as guilty as I am."

Shiloh smiled, "Okay, let's finish dealing with you and then we can talk about me. Get dressed and we'll finish this conversation over dinner. I'm going to get you a room and when I get back, we'll get you settled. I'll change and then we'll head out."

"That's fine," she said with a smile. "Why can't my husband be like you; you just take charge and I love it."

"Shelly, I'm sure your husband is a take-charge kinda person or he wouldn't be wealthy. He just doesn't know how to handle you." Shiloh said with a grin.

Once he secured a room for Shelly and changed his clothes, they headed to dinner and to finish their conversation.

"So, what's her name?" Shelly asked.

Shiloh took a sip of his Pepsi and smiled. "Moselle," he answered.

"And why are you and Moselle not together because your face just lit up when you called her name."

There was a long period of silence before he answered. "I caught her with another man - something I can't forgive or forget."

"Well," Shelly started and then paused to wipe her mouth, "that's rather hypocritical of you, wouldn't you say?"

"Excuse me?" Shiloh asked incredulously.

"How can you say you can't forgive her or forget about finding her with another man when you are in the same boat?"

"Now, hold on a minute," he said, "You and I didn't end up in bed, I put the breaks on, remember?"

"That doesn't matter, Shi, you still entertained the thought and had your hands on my body." Shelly gave him a look that said, Touché!

Shiloh sat back in his chair and crossed his arms over his chest. He couldn't help but smile. "Okay, I'll give you that one, but still."

Shelly sat forward, "But still what? Do you think my husband, if he cared, would think I'd cheated even though you and I didn't actually have intercourse? Would you?" She asked.

After he thought about her question, Shiloh nodded. "I guess you have a point," he said.

"I do have a point and I think you should rethink your position on this whole cheating thing. I understand how you men feel. It's okay if *you* screw around, but if *we* do, we've given away *your* cookie." Her look told him she found that whole idea wrong.

"I'm not like that, Shelly."

"Oh, really? So, if you and Moselle find yourselves back together one day, are you going to tell her about me, or are you going to just expect an apology from her to make things right?"

"Wow . . . I guess I never really thought about it like that."

"Of course you didn't, you're a man and you guys never think of it like that. But we women do and, frankly, we're tired of the double standard."

"Alright, alright. Down girl, I'm not Nik, I'm Shiloh."

"I know who you are . . . very much so."

"So," he started, "If you're so unhappy, why don't you file for divorce and set yourself free?" he asked changing the subject.

"I don't know Shi. If I do, are you gonna be available?"

"No, baby, you know we'd never work. Besides, I'm not the only good man left. There are at least 100 guys out there who'd love to have you."

"And why wouldn't we work?" Shelly asked.

"Because, like you pointed out, my heart belongs to someone else now."

"My life isn't so bad . . ."

Shiloh reached for her hands. "No, it really isn't. You just need to lay some law down with that man of yours. Let him know it's time for him to get his stuff together and mean it. Divorce shouldn't be an option. "

"And how will I do that? He doesn't listen to me nor does he care what I have to say." The dejection was written all over her face.

"Just handle him the way you just handled me. Stop playing soft ball with him. Women play soft ball, men play hard ball. Play the game the way the games being played."

Shelly smiled and nodded. "I like that. Thank you."

He leaned over and kissed her lips one last time, "And thank you."

Chapter 40

"Hey lil' man!" Shiloh greeted his son who toddled over to his dad as fast as his little legs would take him.

Tristan reached his arms into the air, a signal he wanted to be picked up. "Dah dah! Dah dah!" he said, as his father scooped him up.

"Did you miss me?" Shiloh asked as he proceeded to tickle Tristan.

"He sure did," Ines commented.

"Hey Ma, how are you?" Shiloh momentarily turned his attention away from his baby boy and focused on his mother. He leaned down and gave her a kiss on the cheek.

"I'm good baby, how are you?"

"I'm okay," Shiloh answered.

"What's wrong?" Ines asked

"I'm just a little tired. Where's Dad?" Shiloh asked now aware his father was not in the house.

"He went to take our things home."

Shiloh frowned. "Oh, it's like that? Y'all tired of me and Tristan already huh?"

"No baby, of course not, your father and I have a date. Since he's a little slow, he went ahead of me to start getting ready."

"A date! Wow! That's great Ma. You must be more comfortable leaving your two favorite sons alone," he ribbed her.

Ines laughed, "You are so silly. Actually, your father and I decided we need to spend more time enjoying each other, something we seldom do."

"Now, that's the truth. I hope the vacation I sent you on had something to do with this decision of yours."

"It sure does. We enjoyed ourselves and each other so much; we saw what we were missing."

Shiloh smiled and pulled his mother to him in another hug, "That's good stuff Mom; good stuff."

"Daa-ma!" Tristan yelled as he pushed his father away from Ines. "Daama!"

Ines took her grandson from Shiloh and held him tight. "Daa-ma loves this baby, she sure does." She spoke softly to Tristan.

"Lub daa-ma," Tristan repeated back. He clung to her for dear life.

"I think he knows your getting ready to go Ma," Shiloh said. "Do you want me to distract him?"

Ines swallowed the lump growing in her throat. It was more difficult to leave Tristan now that he had gotten older and knew the meaning of goodbye.

"Yeah baby, do that. I can't stand the way he screams anymore when Robert and I leave."

"Okay, I'll take him upstairs and start his bath; he loves the tub, so that should do it."

"Come' on lil' man; lets go get in the tub. How about I do a shower with you. Wanna get in the shower?" Shiloh asked his son as he took him from Ines.

"No! Daa-ma! Daa-ma!" Tristan cried and held tighter to Ines' shirt.

"Oh baby, please don't cry like that, you gonna make Daa-ma cry. I'll give him his bath," Ines said to Shiloh.

"Mother, no you won't. Now, dad is home waiting to take the love of his life out on the town. Tristan will be fine. If you start giving in to him every time he has a hissy fit, you will create a monster."

"But, I can't stand to see him cry like this," she said almost in tears herself. She held her grandson tighter.

"Excuse me?! You ain't have no problem lettin' my butt cry as a child, how you gonna make special exceptions for Tristan?" Shiloh asked incredulously.

"This is different; this is my first grandbaby."

"Give me my son, Mama, and go home and get dressed for dinner or wherever Dad is taking you." Shiloh said and lifted Tristan from Ines' arms.

The toddler took his crying up three decibels and kicking into a tantrum. "Tristan!" Shioh's voice boomed and caused a sudden halt to the baby's noise.

Shiloh held Tristan out from him and looked the little boy straight in the eyes. "Daa-ma has to go home now and you and I are going to get a shower, read a story and go to bed in that order. Now pipe down before your warning becomes something more."

Tristan laid his head on his father's shoulder. His crying became a whimper and he reached his little hand out to his grandmother.

Ines kissed his hand and his cheek and then rolled her eyes at Shiloh. "You got one more time to raise your voice at my grandbaby," she said as she picked her purse up, grabbed her jacket and headed out the door.

"I love you too Ma," Shiloh said and planted a kiss on the top of her head as she exited through the front door.

Two hours later Tristan was clean, read to and fast asleep. Shiloh felt the events of the past couple of days begin to surface in his mind. He thought about Clarence's words and the near mistake with Shelly. He chuckled to himself as he wondered how Clarence knew.

"Guess it's that wisdom that comes with age," he said to himself.

As he lay across his bed, his thoughts turned to Moselle. This time he didn't push them away. After about fifteen minutes of staring at his ceiling fan and reminiscing, he contemplated giving her a call.

His mother's words on forgiveness also came to him, and on a whim, he dialed Ines. Shiloh knew his mother well enough to know her words usually carried some weight. This time he wanted to know what exactly her message on forgiveness was all about.

She answered after about five rings; Shiloh was just about to hang up when Ines picked up. "What is it Son?"

There was so much noise in the background Shiloh could barely hear her. "Mom, where are you?" He asked.

"I'm at a jazz club with your dad down in Ashland. What do you need? I'm missing the show."

"Oh wow, I can talk with you later Mom. Go ahead back with Dad."

"No, because you wouldn't have called me if it wasn't important; now what is it?"

"Your comment on forgiveness - what did you mean by all you said? - you know people making terrible mistakes and needing forgiveness from those they've wronged."

Ines took a minute and stepped outside before she answered. "Shiloh, I'm only going to say this once, so listen closely. Your father and I weren't always as strong as we are now. It came with a lot of hard work and determination to stay together. Part of that hard work began before we were married."

Raising Tristan

"Wait Mom, are you saying Dad cheated on you?" Shiloh sat up in bed.

Ines paused she wanted to intentionally leave her son wondering. "I'm not saying your father cheated on me. I'm just saying in relationships sometimes terrible mistakes are made and if the couple values what God has given them, they have to forgive and move on."

"Mom . . . did you cheat?" he sounded stunned.

"Stop trying to figure things out and listen to the lesson. You have to weigh the relationship for yourself. Is Moselle really the woman God has for you? If so, forgive her. I didn't say forget, I said, forgive. The memory fades with time once forgiveness is released."

There was silence on Shiloh's end of the line. "Son, I have to go now. We can talk more tomorrow if you want. Your father is going to come looking for me if I don't get back."

"Okay, Mom. Thank you and have a good time."

Shiloh lay across the bed a few more minutes and contemplated his mother's words. *"Did my Mom step out on Dad?"* He wondered aloud. He knew that was one question he'd never have answered. Even if he asked his father, he wouldn't get a straight answer. He decided to let that matter go and phone Moselle.

He couldn't say he was surprised when the call went to voice mail, he figured she was with Majid. As he put the phone down, he didn't know if he'd try the call again.

Shiloh rolled over and turned out the light. For now he was going to relax and do something he rarely did, get eight hours of sleep.

Chapter 41

The sound of his cell phone startled Shiloh from a sound sleep. When he glanced at the clock, he realized he'd only been asleep for about twenty minutes. "I must be tired," he said aloud as he reached for the ringing phone.

"Hello?" His tone was groggy.

"I'm sorry, did I wake you? I saw where you called but I can call another time." It was Moselle.

"No, no Mo hey . . . I'm good." he said as he scrambled to turn on the light.

"Ahh, how've you been?" he asked.

"I've been doing well. How are you and how's your son?

We're both doing well. Tristan will be two soon, can you believe it?"

Moselle smiled. "Wow . . . those two years flew by."

There was a period of silence as both contemplated their next words. Moselle spoke first. "Shiloh, I'm so sorry for what I did to you, to us."

He was quiet as he waited for her to continue. "I wasn't thinking clearly, I was caught up. My desire for what I thought could bring me happiness overshadowed what I really wanted."

"And what was that? What did you really want?" He asked.

"You, I wanted you, Shiloh. You have to understand where I came from and what my background is. My parents always pushed me from childhood to marry up."

"Excuse me?!"

"Please let me finish before you say anything; I think you'll understand."

"Okay, go on," he said. His tone was a lot less pleasant that time.

"I come from a well-to-do family and as biased as it may seem, the women in my family have always been encouraged to marry for money."

Moselle paused to take a sip of her water. "When you've heard that nonsense from birth, it's difficult to shake."

"Okay." He acknowledged her statement and then sat upright in bed. "What are you saying?"

"I'm saying I realize I don't have to follow those standards."

"No, you don't but why now? Why has it taken you so long to see that?'

"Shiloh, I not only heard that mess from my mother, but from my aunts as well. I especially heard it from both my grandmothers. That kind of message becomes ingrained and subliminal after a while. You have to understand I not only heard it but saw it demonstrated as well."

"Wow . . . I've been told about such thinking but I've never had it directed at me."

"It's going to take me some time, but I'm working on becoming a better woman."

"I'm sure you'll accomplish all of your goals."

"Shiloh, again I'm so sorry. I pray you find it in your heart to forgive me."

"You know Mo, all of us make mistakes from time to time . . . some worse than others."

"Thanks, I guess." She chuckled.

"Let me finish," he admonished.

"Sorry." He couldn't see her smile but he heard it in her pitch and it made him smile too.

"While we've been apart, I've learned a little more about myself, like the fact I can get caught up in awkward situations too."

She waited.

"I enrolled Tristan in daycare for backup assistance to my parents. The director is an old girlfriend of mine. Anyway, she is married but I found myself becoming involved with her."

"Oh really?" Moselle's tone revealed her surprise at his honesty.

"Yes, really, and it taught me a valuable lesson. We never slept together, but we came pretty close."

"It seems like we both have some growing to do," Moselle said.

"Mo, listen. I never stopped thinking about you. I know you made your decision, but I want you to know that."

"Majid and I are no longer seeing each other, Shiloh. Once I admitted to myself I was in it for all the wrong reasons, I got out."

"Listen; is it possible I can see you sometime soon? There are some things I'd like to say to you but not over the phone."

"Okay, I'm free today and tomorrow but I work next weekend. That's unless you want to meet sometime during the week."

Shiloh thought quickly about his schedule for that Saturday. He knew he had some things to take care of around the house and grocery shopping later that afternoon, but he didn't want to delay his talk with Moselle.

"Can you meet for brunch at about eleven o'clock tomorrow?"

"That's fine. I have a few errands to run but I can get an early start and finish after we meet up."

Just then, Shiloh heard, Tristan cry out. "Hey babe, I think Tristan's having a bad dream. I gotta run but I'll see you tomorrow. How about we meet at *Millie's Diner* in the *Bottom*?"

"That'll work. Good night."

"Good night." Shiloh couldn't help but smile. He jumped out of bed and headed into his son's room.

"Coming Tristan!"

Chapter 42

"Thanks for watching Tristan for me Mom." Shiloh hugged his mother in gratitude.

"Not a problem, you know we love spending time with our grandson."

"Great, I'll be back as soon as I can."

"Don't rush; take your time." Ines smiled. Tell Moselle I said hello."

Shiloh frowned. "How did you know I'm meeting Mo? Then again, don't bother answering that question."

Raising Tristan

"Now see." Ines picked Tristan up and headed into the kitchen. "You think it's because I know things sometimes, but this is different. It's written all over your face."

He grinned. "How so?"

"Shiloh baby, Moselle is the only woman you've ever loved who makes your face light up when you even think of her."

Twenty minutes later, Shiloh pulled up to *Mille's Diner* and handed his keys to the Valet. He hurried inside to put his name on the list to be seated and then went back to the door to watch for Moselle. She wasn't very far behind him, and when he saw her she left him breathless.

Moselle's hair had been cut in a short bob that complimented her heart shaped face. She wore a red coat with large black buttons that hit right at her waist and allowed Shiloh an unobstructed view of her shapely derrière when she turned to the Valet.

Her jewelry and makeup complimented her Cafe Au Lait complexion perfectly. Shiloh felt as though he were seeing her for the first time. When Moselle turned and found him in him door, her face broke into a broad grin.

- 225 -

"Thanks for meeting me," Shiloh said over brunch.

"I'm happy I did," Moselle replied.

"Mo, I know it's been awhile, but like I said on the phone, I never stopped thinking of you."

She blushed and looked down. "I never stopped thinking of you either."

"What I'd like to do is start over. I'm not making any promises; let's just see where it goes." He looked into her eyes to gauge her response.

"I'd like that, she responded.

"Great!" He extended his hand and said, "Hi beautiful, my name is Shiloh Milner, what's yours?"

Chapter 43

Moselle stood facing the man who in a matter of minutes would become her husband. As she heard the minister speaking her full name, expecting her to repeat after him, she did so on autopilot.

"I, Moselle Renae Laveau . . ." As the words left her mouth, her eyes never left her intended. She took in the full features of his face. The way soft lines framed his brown eyes as he smiled, the length of his nose speaking to his Creole heritage and his full lips that left her breathless so many times, when he kissed her.

Still, she wondered how she had gotten there. How had this man come into her life so unexpectedly and swept her off her feet. He was not the type of man she anticipated spending her life with.

He wasn't a doctor or accountant or a shirt-and-tie kinda guy, yet he was all she'd ever wanted. On any given day she would have passed him by, but something about him made it impossible to walk away.

When she heard the familiar voice of his three year old son, her focus momentarily shifted to the front pew where the boy sat with her future in-laws. Moselle couldn't help but smile.

Shiloh beamed at his fiancé making eye contact with his son. He couldn't believe she was really standing face to face with him, pledging her love for eternity. He gently squeezed her diminutive hand, drawing her attention back to him.

There was a period of time in their relationship when he surmised things between them were over. But the bond between them prevailed, and now she was becoming his wife.

"By the power and authority invested in me by God and the State of Louisiana, I now pronounce you husband and wife together. Shiloh, you may salute your bride."

As Shiloh pulled Moselle into his arms, he felt as though he was in a fairytale. His life was finally perfect. He had finally arrived. "I love you, Mo," he whispered into her lips as he kissed his new wife.

"I love you more," she answered. When they finally pulled away from one another and faced the congregation, the applause was thunderous.

Shiloh scooped his son into his left arm and used his right arm to draw Mo to him. They were now a family, and he knew God had blessed him with more than he'd ever dreamt possible.

Chapter 44

Twelve years later . . .

"I'll get it Mom! Tristan yelled to Moselle.

At age fifteen, he was the splitting image of his father. He stood five foot eleven inches tall with the same mahogany brown skin, full lips and slender nose. The only feature Tristan possessed that didn't remind one of his father was his piercing brown eyes. The attentive manner in which Shiloh groomed, Tristan made sure he was on his way to becoming just as conscientious as himself.

Moselle and Shiloh often left Tristan in charge of his younger eleven year old twin sisters, Maya and Amelia when they had date night - a responsibility Tristan took seriously.

A few seconds later Moselle heard the alarm system chime as the front door opened, but she didn't hear Tristan announce the visitor. "Who is it, Tristan?"

When he didn't respond, she asked again. "Tristan, I asked who is at the door?" Moselle called out from the laundry room.

She knew that although he was only fifteen, Tristan was her most dependable child. When she got no response the second time, Moselle became concerned. She looked at Amelia who was helping her out and then placed the clean clothes in her hands back into the dryer and headed to the door.

Just as she turned the corner from the kitchen into the hallway leading to foyer, she heard Maya say, "I think it's his mother."

The End . . . Or is it?

Savannah J

Savannah J. was born and raised in Wilmington, Delaware in an Italian neighborhood affectionately referred to as "Little Italy". The unconditional love and support of her family and influence of her environment fostered her love and talents in the Arts. Subsequently, during her college years, she studied music and literature, which fed her passion for writing. She is the author of "Toward the Light" and the sequel "The Prodigal Son," "Behind Closed Doors," and The Prey. She was also the founder and organizer and host of The Annual Authors Literary Festival, which was held in the Richmond Virginia Metro Area for over four years. It is her goal to one day host the event again.

Savannah J. currently resides in Virginia with her son and family. For more information see her website at www.thesavannahjpublications.com or email her at savnhj@aol.com. "Toward the Light" is available at www.authorhouse.com. "The Prey" and "Raising Tristan" are available through Savannah's website and in eBook on Amazon and Google Play Books.

Savannah J

Raising Tristan

www.ingramcontent.com/pod-product-compliance
Lightning Source LLC
Chambersburg PA
CBHW072231170626
46813CB00003B/1174